BAD JUSTICE

AN UNCANNY INK STORY

DAVID BUSSELL
M.V. STOTT

BECOME AN INSIDER

Sign up and receive **FREE UNCANNY KINGDOM BOOKS**. Also, be the **FIRST** to hear about **NEW RELEASES** and **SPECIAL OFFERS** in the **UNCANNY KINGDOM** universe. Just visit:

WWW.UNCANNYKINGDOM.COM

BAD
JUSTICE

1

Look, I'll be the first to admit it, I have my flaws. Flaws and imperfections so tiny, so absolutely miniscule, that I'm sure they're barely even noticeable to most people. For example, I pick the skin around my fingernails habitually. Honest to god, the tips of my fingers look like they've been sucked on by a zombie. Half of the reason my hands are always in fists is because I'm hiding my knackered nails. The other half is because I like punching people, which is definitely not a flaw.

Then there's my love of Jason Statham movies. Say what you like, but I love that bald, grunting, high-kicking man. I once smacked a bloke in the crotch for bad-mouthing *Transporter 3,* and that one's not even all that good.

What else do you need to know about me...?

Oh, right, I murder people.

A lot.

Like, a lot-a lot.

Since getting into the Uncanny world I've lost count of the number of people I've put in pine boxes. I'd say I'm not proud of that, but that would be a big fat lie. Each of those coffins represents a job successfully completed, and each completion means I get to charge more for my services. And I love me some filthy lucre. *Love it.* Disney could make a movie about my relationship with money, a real fairy tale. Let it be known that I, Erin Banks, get wet for money.

Wait, that makes me sound like a prostitute. I'm not a prostitute, I just kill for cash, which is, uh, better? Worse? Where was I going with this whole imperfections thing anyway...?

Oh!

That was it.

I'm totally shit with money. Love it to bits but can't keep hold of it. It's only a matter of weeks since the whole Galoffi kidnapping thing and I've already burned through that pay day. To be fair, a lot of that has been spent paying off debts that I'd built up before I was sent to prison. I also fixed up the Porsche a little that I'd, well, *liberated* from that hot bastarding bastard, Kirklander.

He did send a few texts enquiring about the where-abouts of his car, to which I'd replied that it was now mine in return for what he'd done to me (the whole prison thing). I also explained that if he attempted to reclaim the vehicle I would tear off his balls and stuff them so far down his throat that he'd get a following on Porn Hub.

The Porsche remained mine.

He never actually brought up the fact I'd recently kicked the snot out of him, then knocked him unconscious with his own magical staff. I think he took the car thing much more personally. He might be a complete prick, but even he knows he didn't get anything he wasn't begging for. Even if he'd managed to get the soul before me, he'd have known it was only a matter of time before I knocked him uncon-scious, or worse. A price he was willing to pay for a job he saw as fair game. To him, *every* bounty is fair game, no matter what. We weren't in the business of honour, we were in the business of getting paid.

So, money was too tight to mention, and I was back at Parker's—my tattoo guy, friend, and kinda agent—trying to hustle up a new gig. Booze doesn't pay for itself, you know. Well, except for that time I accepted a spell by way of payment; one that fooled the barman over at Baker's Pub into thinking that I'd already paid each time I ordered a drink. Unfortunately, that wore off after one blissful, fairly hazy week, and he barred me for the rest of the month. Bit of an overreaction if you ask me, especially considering all the money I'd shovelled into the place over the years. Sure, the spell had the side effect of making him lose all of his hair, but I fail to see how he could blame me for that, it's not like I created the bloody thing.

Anyway. Back to Parker's tattoo joint, where I was experiencing the familiar agony of the needle.

'Christ,' I grunted through clenched teeth as the tattoo gun in Parker's hand stabbed my skin over and over, turning me into a blood-streaked pin cushion.

'Welcome back, girl,' he chirped. 'You were out of it for a while there.'

'What?'

'You blacked out. Dead to the world.'

'No I did not,' I replied all cotton-mouthed and woozy.

'Yeah, you did,' Parker replied, a pure white light seeping from his sightless eyes, coiling in ribbons down his arm and into the needle that impregnated my flesh.

The pain was incredible, but it was worth it. Once Parker was done and the ink had bedded in, I'd be back to my old self, leaching magic from the air around me and doing all kinds of superpowered shit.

My whole body was a clenched talon, but I couldn't have Parker seeing the pain I was in. I breathed deep and slow, straining to keep my muscles relaxed, desperate not to show him how much I was hurting, determined not to pass out again.

'There, all done.'

I sagged in relief as Parker lifted his foot off the pedal and the tattoo needle ceased its assault.

'How was the pain today?' he asked, the ribbons of light recoiling up his arm and seeping back into his milk-white eyes.

'Barely even noticed it,' I lied, expertly.

'You're obviously lying, girl, unless you suddenly turned narcoleptic.'

Parker might be blind on paper, but nothing gets past him. Somehow. I've never been all that clear on the details; he was frustratingly vague about just how it was he could see despite having no eyesight.

'I can handle it,' I said, wincing as I used shaky arms to push myself up into a sitting position, swallowing down a little sick that lurched its way up my throat. Parker tossed me a towel and I dabbed tenderly at my blood-slicked arms and shoulders, my skin feeling like I'd just taken a nap on a barbecue grill.

The tattoos he gave me were the reason I was able to operate in the Uncanny world and do the dangerous job that I do. Unfortunately for me I was born a "normal": a word used to describe those of us born without a connection to magic. It's also a word that will get you kicked in the nuts if you ever aim it in my direction.

I take no pride in being a muggle. Because I wasn't born to the Uncanny, the powers Parker gives me weaken over time before my body finally rejects them entirely. That compatibility problem is why I spend half of my life lying in his tattoo chair getting my ink refreshed, biting my tongue and lapsing into unconsciousness. That pain, the byproduct of painting my body with arcane symbols, of meddling with occult forces I should be no part of, follows me out of the tattoo parlour too. It's a pain that's ever-present, stinging my flesh, burning like hot daggers. My bones ache constantly and I get migraines so bad I think my head's going to split in half. As a result of all that, I've taken to self-medicating with alcohol and painkillers. Look out for me in a future AA meeting, coming your way soon!

Anyway, what's life without a little (or in my case, a shit-tonne) of pain? What do you mean, *'It's wonderful'*? Shut your face.

'You could always give up this line of work and go back to what you should be,' said Parker, shrugging and making his pineapple sprout of dreadlocks bob to and fro.

'It's very rude of you to make assumptions about what I'm brooding over,' I replied, wincing as I put my bra and t-shirt back on. 'Anyway, these things on my arms were your idea in the first place, or has that slipped your mind?'

'I'm just saying, girl, there are plenty of jobs out there that don't ask you to damage yourself. That don't include murder and mayhem and blood and guts.'

'Christ, that sounds boring.'

'Yeah, but you'll live longer.'

'Has Lana been bending your ear?'

'Your cousin is wiser than you.'

'My cousin is a Transformer that got stuck as a family hatchback.'

Parker grinned. 'Makes great lemon drizzle cake, though. I go through that shit like crack.'

Although that was true, I wouldn't take Lana's life over

mine if Jason Statham offered it to me on a silver platter. Not even if he was naked and greased up like he is that fight scene from the first *Transporter* movie. Oh man, I'm going to be thinking about that all day now.

I stepped down from the tattoo chair and slumped on the couch. 'I don't know if you've forgotten, Parks, but I basically work for you. You're my agent in chaos. If I don't kill people, you don't get paid.'

He snorted and shook his head. 'I've got others on the books, I'll be fine. You might not be. Who knows what long-term damage I'm doing to you here.'

'Damage? I've never felt better,' I replied, feeling about eighty.

'Okay, you're the boss, but don't come running to me when you're dead at thirty.'

'I promise I won't do that.'

I crossed my arms in a huff. Parker was my friend, but he was also the guy I relied on for work. What I needed from him was a new contract, not the fatherly concern act. I already had one shitty dad, I didn't need another.

'So, what have you got for me?' I asked.

'What makes you think I got anything?'

'Don't fuck about, Parks. I've been living on baked beans and porridge for the last week. Get me some money, momma needs a fat stack, pronto.'

Parker frowned. 'Well, I might have something.'

'Ooh!' I replied, sitting forward, a fresh tingle of excitement momentarily pushing down the pain of my freshly-carved tattoos.

'Just cool it, I said I might have something.'

I failed to cool it.

'What is it? An assassination job? I could really go for a bit of murder right now. Something really icky. Something where I'll still be finding dried blood under my nails a week later.'

Parker laughed and shook his head. 'Yeah, you ain't gonna be able to leave this world behind, are you?'

'I'm a sick puppy, dude. Now gimme the details so I can put on my best murder trousers.'

'The job's not ready.'

'Aw, come on, just give me a sniff.'

'I have to go through official channels on this one. Can't say any more until the ink's dry, you get me?'

I flopped back again. 'Well, that ink had better dry quick, I'm bored shitless. I've actually started to miss prison. At least in there the constant threat of extreme violence keeps you on your toes.'

'You need help.'

'I need work.'

My phone rang, I reached into the pocket of my jeans to find a familiar name beaming from the screen.

'Parker, have you and Lana been conspiring to double-up the pressure or what?'

He lifted both hands in an '*I'm innocent*' gesture.

I raised an eyebrow in his direction and hit Answer. 'What's up, cuz? You can save the concern, I'm beyond help.'

'Erin... I'm at the hospital. You need to come, now.'

My whole body turned cold. I was out of the door a second later.

2

I stood at the far end of the Royal Sussex County Hospital car park, nervously passing my phone from one hand to the other like it was burning my palms.

I hadn't brought it up with Parker while he was busy riding my hump, but there was another reason I stayed in the Uncanny world beyond the sheer thrill of it. A reason I had no choice but to stay for. A reason he knew all too well.

My brother.

James Banks had been taken from me when he was just a baby. Taken by something out of the ordinary. Something Uncanny. I know because I saw it happen. James' disappearance was what opened my eyes to the magic and monsters around me. To the secret world that lived right next to mine, sight unseen. A world I made myself a part of to escape the real world, and for a more important reason: to discover what had happened to my little brother. To find out who took him and why.

To get revenge.

James' disappearance turned the world upside down. Ruined everything. Pulled my family inside-out. The way my mum and dad have treated me since James was taken has been... well, let's just say it hasn't been nice. Some— such as my cousin Lana—might say the more-than-frosty relationship I have with my parents is at least partially, *partially*, down to how off the rails I went after James was taken. Deep down I knew there was some truth to that, but I was never going to admit it, least of all to my parents. Far as I was concerned, they'd had their chance. Lana was all the family I needed now.

The automatic doors at the front of the hospital swished open and Lana stepped out, scanning the car park, one hand over her eyes like a sailor scanning for icebergs. I waved to catch her attention. She flapped a hand back and made a beeline in my direction.

Lana.

The only member of my sad little clan that I still had any sort of contact with. The only one I trusted and could admit that I loved. Lana knew everything about me, about what I did. Well, more or less everything. I mean, she didn't know that I once broke a guy's neck because he told me I should smile more. Lana's understanding enough, but I was sure to get the whole Judge Judy routine over that one.

'Erin,' said Lana, her eyes red from crying. She always was overly-emotional.

'Jesus, you look fucking awful,' I said, rarely the overly-supportive sort.

Lana laugh-snorted and reached into a pocket for a tissue to wipe her nose with. She smoothed down her long, blonde hair, tidying herself up a bit. 'I wasn't sure you'd come,' she said, pocketing the gooey tissue.

I'd surprised myself at how quickly I left Parker's to get to the hospital, considering the circumstances.

'Well, how is the wicked witch?' I asked.

'She's still unconscious,' replied Lana.

I nodded and frowned, perching on the low wall behind me and kicking the heels of my battered boots against it.

'She's your mother,' said Lana, hopping up on the wall beside me, 'you should go in and see her.'

'No, I really, really shouldn't.'

'Your dad just nipped home to get some things for her, no one will know.'

'*I'll* know,' I replied.

'Your mum's been in a car crash. She's really bad, Erin.'

That's what Lana had told me over the phone that got me out of Parker's so fast. Still, I'd almost pulled the car over three times on the way over. Almost turned around to go, well, anywhere else. So Mum was in hospital? So what? She wasn't dead. And even if she was...

I bit my lip as all sorts of conflicting emotions fought a battle royale inside me.

'It's the right thing to do, Erin,' said Lana, 'go in and see her.'

'The right thing? When has that ever had anything to do with me? I once killed a man with his own tongue, did I ever tell you that? Tore it out at the root and stuffed it down his throat so he choked to death. You should have seen the look on his face.'

'Have you finished? Erin, you know you want to see her, so just see her.'

I gazed towards the hospital. 'What's the point?'

'You'll feel better knowing you did.'

'No, I won't.'

'Erin—'

I turned on her, a snarl upon my lips. 'You know better than anyone how that bitch treated me. So she crashed her car and broke a few bones, big whoop, who gives a shit? I'm supposed to just push everything that's happened aside and act like nothing's wrong? Like she didn't... like she didn't...'

I wanted to say, '*Like she didn't turn me into this,*' but I had too much pride.

I scratched at the tattoos Parker had given me, causing my skin to sting sharply. We sat in silence for a while while I pushed down the guilt I felt for yelling at Lana. Lana who was kindness incarnate. Lana who'd do anything for me, and had done on many occasions.

'Sorry,' I mumbled quietly.

Lana laid her head on my shoulder. 'That's okay, cuz. I'll always be here for you to shout at.'

That didn't make me feel any better.

I was sat brooding in Baker's Pub, slouched on a bar stool among a minefield of empty pint glasses. I'd been there a couple of hours already, and so far the alcohol was doing a terrible job of calming me down. A couple more and I'd be back in the zone though, I was sure of it.

'Another one here, mate,' I said, waggling my empty glass in the barman's direction.

Looked like his hair was starting to come back. Only took three years.

I pulled out my phone and sent Parker yet another message, asking about the new job he was supposed to be putting together. I needed it desperately. For the money. For the distraction. What better way to bury the stupid emotions trying to claw their way out of my brain grave than by hurling myself into the jaws of peril?

'Hey, there,' said a voice I didn't recognise.

I turned to see a man, mid-thirties, with shaggy dark hair and the misplaced confidence of a bloke five drinks deep.

'Get lost,' I replied.

His face faltered for a second before he rebounded. 'Can I, uh, get you a drink?'

The barman placed my just-ordered pint in front of me.

'I'm all good here.'

The man dithered as he tried to think of what to say next.

'I'll make this easy for you, mate,' I said, 'go away now or I will punch you in the throat.'

The man went away.

My phone buzzed. A message from Parker: *Where you at, girl?*

My heart leapt and I messaged back: *At church. Is the job ready?*

I stared at the phone for several minutes, willing him to answer. He did not answer.

It was just starting to get dark outside, and the chances of the job dropping in my lap before the day was done seemed dim. Looked like I was going to have to stick with using giant amounts of booze as my emotion-muffler.

I downed half the pint in one and let loose a burp of such ferocity that it would have rendered anyone within a foot of me unconscious.

'Fuck,' I grumbled, upset that as much as I drank, as much as I tried to keep my thoughts elsewhere, the same picture kept forcing itself to the front of my mind.

A hospital bed.

My mum, small, broken, unconscious, tubes jabbed into her, the only thing keeping her company the steady *beep-beep-beep* of a heart monitor. Why was I so disturbed by that image? So upset? My mum didn't deserve my worry. I wouldn't be surprised if she'd been more upset at the idea of me visiting her than by the accident itself.

Was that fair? Maybe not. But since when did my thoughts about that woman have to be fair?

I swore as I realised my eyes were getting wet. Fuck that.

'Oi, Shaggy,' I yelled across the pub at the guy who'd tried chatting me up.

He looked over to me, eyes wide, pointing at himself. 'Me?'

'Yeah, you. It's your lucky day, I've decided you can buy me a drink.'

Twenty minutes later the toilet cubicle door slammed closed behind us. One of his hands fumbled the lock into place while the other fumbled at my bra strap.

'I'm, uh, John, by the way,' he mumbled as I chewed on his neck.

'Couldn't give a shit,' I replied, and shoved my tongue into his mouth.

I didn't have a job to distract me, and alcohol wasn't doing the job, so this would have to do. Losing myself to lust. A stupid, desperate hook-up in a pub toilet with a randy random. I'd lose myself in his flesh. Give in to the eager hands that roamed over my body, that groped at my chest and kneaded my arse.

I reached down and grabbed hold of the bulge straining inside his jeans. He let out a yelp of surprise and hopped back.

'You're not gonna get shy on me now, are you?' I asked, grinning as I undid his belt, unbuttoned his jeans.

The man—what was his name again? James? Jason?—shook his head and lunged for my mouth again. He wanted me. He was going to have me. That's all that mattered right there, right then. Not my mum, not my missing brother, not anything.

There was a knock on the outside of the cubicle door.

'Obviously occupied!' I said, unbuttoning my jeans, ready to yank them down.

A second knock.

'Are you stupid, mate? Piss off.'

With a loud crack, the hinges were torn from the cubicle's cheap wooden frame and the door wrenched away to reveal a man so large I took him for a semi-shaved yeti. Despite his imposing bulk and terrible manners he was dressed like a gentleman in an expensive dark blue suit and tie. He offered a nod of his meaty head.

I recognised him.

He worked for Jenkins & Jenkins, defence lawyers for the Uncanny Courts.

'All right, Alan,' I said.

'What the fuck is going on?' asked my bewildered hookup—John, that was it!—no doubt taking this hulking beast for a scorned boyfriend.

Alan placed a finger to his lips then grabbed John by the collar and removed him from the cubicle. Alan wasn't always in control of his own strength, and this was one of those occasions. Instead of pulling John out of the cubicle and pushing him to one side, he accidentally propelled him across the bathroom and landed him in the sinks. A mirror shattered and rained down on my not-quite-lover, tinkling off the bathroom's tile floor.

'Ow...' he managed to say, dazed but not too badly hurt.

'Bad Alan,' I said, wagging a finger at him.

He frowned and pulled out a pad of paper. The word *Sorry* appeared on the page. He tore it off and handed it to John.

Alan was mute, but had the ability to make his thoughts appear on paper without the need of a pencil or pen. It's not the most amazing use of magic you'll see in the Uncanny Kingdom, but it always tickled me, kind of like the first time I saw an Etch A Sketch in action.

'Well?' I said, buttoning my jeans and stepping out of the cubicle, glass crunching beneath my battered black boots.

Alan lifted up another page of his pad: *Parker said you'd be here. You are needed. Follow.*

Alan put the pad away and left the bathroom.

'Sorry, John, duty calls,' I said with a shrug.

He looked up at me with a combination of hurt, confusion, and anger. A difficult mix to pull off, but bless him, he managed it.

I turned away from my would-be shag and followed Alan.

Yup, this was definitely a better distraction than terrible, short-lived toilet sex.

3

Alan drove a big black SUV with blue LED underbody lights and spinning, chrome rims.

Alan was a fancy bitch.

A fancy, tacky, mute bitch.

I hopped into the spacious rear of the car as Alan started the engine and the motor roared into life.

A job for the Uncanny Courts? It had been a long time. Up until this point I'd assumed I was blackballed by the Courts after fucking up so badly on the last job I'd done in that arena (long story short, the bloke I mentioned before that I choked with his own tongue wasn't the right guy). Seemed I'd been let back in the club house, though.

Okay, time for a little info dump.

The ordinary world—the regular United Kingdom—is governed by a single set of laws. The same isn't true for my version of the world. The Uncanny Kingdom is a jumbled-up jigsaw, and few of the pieces fit together right. Each province has different laws, different means of justice. The laws of some places, like London, are left entirely in the hands of a coven of witches and their familiar. They're considered the highest form of justice, and it's up to them to keep order and punish anyone that steps out of line.

In Brighton, things are a little bit different. There's no coven looking over East Sussex, so an Uncanny Court was formed to stop the county turning into the wild west. In many ways it's just like the court of law you're familiar with, only it deals entirely with Uncanny folk.

Oh, and within this system of law, it's an entirely legitimate tactic to murder a court witness.

By which I mean you can silence those suckers before they get anywhere near a courthouse. Legally and permanently. Hey, don't ask me, a bunch of wizards wrote the rules about five-hundred years ago. Take it up with those beardy-weirdy fuckers if you don't like it.

Anyway, like I was saying, according to our laws, if a witness is found before a court case gets rolling, the defence is entirely in their right to kill them. And that's where folks like me come in. The defence—in this case, Jenkins & Jenkins—can hire an assassin to off the troublesome witness whose testimony might land their clients in prison. It sounds crazy, but for someone in my line of work, working the Uncanny Court is as close to a legit, punching the clock office job as I'm likely to get.

I shuffled forward on the leather seat of the SUV. 'Any idea what the job is?' I asked my burly driver.

Alan lifted the pad over his shoulder: *Nope*.

'Always a pleasure, Alan.'

Yup.

Ten minutes later we pulled up outside the offices of Jenkins & Jenkins. The practice was housed on the third floor of an ordinary-looking office building. An everyday, bread and butter law firm lived on the fifth floor. I often wondered if they had any inkling of an idea what kind of waters Jenkins & Jenkins waded through.

The lift pinged and the doors slid open, delivering me to the reception desk where I was greeted by Olivia, the firm's receptionist, perched behind her desk with her hair in a tight, blonde bun, a sour look on her face.

'Oh, it's you,' she said.

'I hope so.'

'I thought you were in jail,' she said, squinting her piggy eyes.

'I was. Now I'm not.'

'Good for you,' she replied, her face a mask of barely-concealed contempt.

Olivia had never been my biggest fan. I think it was my snogging the face off her boyfriend at the office Christmas party three years previous that had done it. In my defence, I only did it to annoy her. I guess it's not much of a defence, now I come to think of it.

Tell them, said Alan's pad of paper.

Olivia grimaced at me as she pressed the intercom.

'Olivia?' came the voice of Jenkins. Or maybe it was Jenkins, they did sound very similar.

'Ellen is here,' she said, all chirpy.

'Erin,' I replied.

'Send her in,' said Jenkins. Or Jenkins.

'You can go through, Ellen,' said Olivia with an expression that suggested I'd just farted and followed through.

'Thanks,' I replied and stepped towards the door. 'Oh, how's Mike, by the way?'

Alan's back shielded me from the stapler that was launched in my direction.

'Thanks, big man.'

Welcome.

We stepped into the office and Alan took up a post in the corner of the room.

The office stank of mahogany and cigars. Bookcases strained under the weight of hundreds of hardback legal books so hefty that just one of them would have been sufficient to stun a whale. Oil paintings of the Jenkins brothers dominated the wall behind two, large, solid desks, each with a plush, dark green leather chair.

'Erin! Come in, take a seat. So good to have you out of jail and back breaking necks,' said Jenkins.

'Thanks, though I do miss showering in front of fifty violent women.'

The other Jenkins laughed and poured me a glass of water. 'So, a lot of lesbian action in there? How much? A lot, yes?' His brother tossed a sour look in his direction. 'I'm only asking!'

This is going to get really confusing really fast, so here's what we'll do: there are two Jenkins. They're brothers, twins. I don't know their first names, no one does. From here on in I'll refer to them as "Alive Jenkins" and "Dead Jenkins".

Alive Jenkins was alive. He was in his mid-sixties, fleshy with old age, and down to a horseshoe of white hair. A wispy silver moustache sat beneath his gout-red nose. He looked as though he might have a heart attack if forced to tackle more than four consecutive stairs.

Dead Jenkins was dead. A ghost. He died in mysterious circumstances when he was thirty-six, and looked just as he had at the point of his death. Full head of thick, dark hair, clean shaven, slim and toned. Kind of a looker.

This difference in their appearance, and life status, was a constant point of contention between the two. Alive Jenkins resented that he looked like refried crap, while his twin looked at his peak, despite the march of time. Dead Jenkins resented the fact that his twin was alive and could indulge in the plea-sures of sin—food, booze, women, men—Alive Jenkins did it all, and took great relish in telling Dead Jenkins all about it.

Alive Jenkins handed me the glass of water. 'We get this from a stream deep beneath the earth that is believed to be the purest water in existence. Isn't it wonderful?'

Dead Jenkins frowned and eyed his brother evilly.

I shrugged. 'Yeah, it's definitely watery,' I replied, wishing someone would pour me a tumbler of something brown.

'I think I'd die if I couldn't enjoy a refreshing glass of ice cold water on a warm summer's day,' said Alive Jenkins, smacking his lips.

'Take a look in a mirror,' said Dead Jenkins, 'it's going to take more than a splash of water to rejuvenate your with-ered old bones.'

'At least I have bones. You're about as solid as a burp in the wind.'

They always did this. How they managed to continue to run their firm was well beyond me.

'Erin,' said Dead Jenkins, 'did my brother here ever tell you about the time he pissed his trousers because he has such a weak, fragile excuse for a body?'

'Don't think so,' I said, sipping my water.

Alive Jenkins rounded on him, his already-red face flushing a darker shade of crimson. 'I have a medical condition!'

'Yes. Piss-pants-itus.'

'I had full sex last night!'

That wiped the smile from Dead Jenkins' phantom face.

'Oh yes. Some first class intercourse. With a woman. My penis felt very good. Oh, very good, indeed.'

'You always go to sex!'

'That's because I have sex. A lot of it. Whether I want to or not, just so I can tell you about it.'

I held up my hands as Alive Jenkins and Dead Jenkins threatened to get into a fight. If that was actually possible. 'Boys, boys, let's stay on track, shall we?' I said. The brothers harrumphed. Once I saw that they weren't about to start tearing strips off each other, I continued. 'Before we go on, I've got two questions.'

Alive Jenkins turned back to me. 'Are either of them about all the sex I can have because my penis isn't made of smoke?'

'I think you already know that they aren't.'

'What are the questions?' asked Dead Jenkins, self-consciously cupping his hands in front of his ghost-crotch.

'Number one, what's the job?'

'Three witnesses need taking care of,' replied Dead Jenkins.

Three? That was a nice amount of murder to keep me occupied, and also it meant three bounties. This was definitely worth abandoning toilet sex with a stranger for.

'Okay,' I replied. 'Question number two: what's that piece of shit doing here?'

I pointed to the so far unmentioned fifth person in the room, sat quietly in the corner of the office sipping a very pure glass of water.

'Erin Banks. We meet again.'

His name was Sallow, and he was dressed entirely in soft black leather. His eyes were like ice-chips, his head shaved to the bone except for a razor-thin stripe that ran from front to back. His face was covered in an assortment of metal studs. He looked a bit like Pinhead from the *Hellraiser* movies, only with a touch more hair and less extreme hood ornaments.

'Do you two know each other?' asked Dead Jenkins.

'This guy?' I cried. 'You invited *this guy* to the party?'

'He's very good at his job,' replied Alive Jenkins.

'We've used him several times in your absence,' added Dead Jenkins.

Sallow was not a pleasant fellow. He was a deviant. A turd in leather. A complete and total wanker. And what's worse, he was the most boring person I'd ever met. How do you dress up like that and still have the personality of a three-week-old shite?

'It's only three witnesses,' I said, 'I don't need help. Leave the tit in leather underpants out of it and I'll take a ten percent cut on the bounty. Can't say fairer than that.'

'Ah, well, the thing is, the case has been bumped up,' said Dead Jenkins. 'It wasn't supposed to start for a month, in which case we'd only have employed one of you, but the case before it fell apart,'

'How long?' I asked.

'The job must be complete by midnight on Wednesday,' replied Alive Jenkins.

'This Wednesday? It's already Monday evening!'

Not a lot of time to track down and kill three witnesses. Three witnesses that the prosecution knew were in the sniper sight, and would be going out of their way to keep safe. Given the tight time frame I could see the sense in bringing in a second party, but it still stung to know that Jenkins & Jenkins didn't trust me to get the job done on my own.

'Okay, fine, two of us. But that pasty git had better stay out of my way or I'll turn his skin into a nice leather jumpsuit and wear it to his funeral.'

'No,' replied Sallow, 'I believe it is you, and not, in fact, I, that should stay out of the way. Or I will kill you. And I will also do something to your skin. Something horrible.'

'I'll pop your eyeball out, squat over your head, and fill your skull with my hot, fresh piss.'

'No. I will do that to you rather than you to me, for I am Sallow.'

'Snappy comeback. You've done lots of crowd work, have you?'

Alive Jenkins coughed. 'If you're quite done...'

I turned in his direction. 'What?'

'We never said we were hiring just *two* people. This is a big case and we have very little time to make sure it goes our way. There are three witnesses, so we've hired three assassins to make sure the job gets done.'

'Three? Who else have you...?' A very bad feeling began to creep over me. 'No. No, no, no. Don't tell me you've hired him... anyone but him.'

The office door opened to reveal a very handsome, grinning man in an ivory-coloured coat that reached almost to the ground. In his hand he held a gnarled wooden staff.

'Hey, baby, how's things?' asked Kirklander.

I turned to Sallow. 'I take it back. Please kill me now.'

4

The atmosphere in the back of Alan's SUV as he drove us out of town was a tad strained, I can tell you.

'You look great,' said Kirklander.

'You don't,' I replied. It was a lie. He looked sexy as fuck, like always. Damn that fine-looking bastard.

The three of us shared the back seat—me, Kirklander and Sallow—three assassins sat awkwardly together as our ride left Brighton behind and took us to the person we'd been hired to exonerate. I was on one side, Kirklander the other, Sallow playing piggy in the middle.

A little info on Sallow. His Uncanny power wasn't just to look sickly and gross in leather bondage gear, although he had a clear gift for it. He also had the ability to drain the strength from his victims with a touch. If he laid his bare hands on a person and willed them to go down, even the strongest man would find himself crumbling to the ground, gasping for breath, unable to summon the power to fight back. After that, all Sallow had to do was stick in the knife.

Don't get me wrong, he's not so tough. Yeah, he's got

some game, but compared to Kirklander and me, he was a bottom-feeder. He didn't have the background we had, didn't have the experience, the résumé. Quite honestly, it was kind of insulting that he'd been put on a job with us.

'Since when did you start getting calls from the Jenkins?' I asked.

'I am Sallow. All know of me. All want to work with me.'

'Yeah, that's not an answer.'

'People fear me. They tremble at the sound of my name. Their bowels loosen when they hear talk of my coming.'

'How. Long. You. Boring. Tit.'

Sallow frowned and shifted in the seat. 'Since last month.'

'How did you swing that?' I asked.

'I swung it, for I am Sallow. The one all fear.'

'Hey, milky, do you also have the Uncanny ability to drain the life out of a conversation?'

Kirklander smirked and it annoyed me how much pleasure his reaction gave me.

'Do not test me, girl,' said Sallow.

'Or what? You'll carry on talking to me?'

'No, I'll... that is to say... you will beg for death because—'

'What? What will you do?'

'I am Sallow.'

'Sorry, what was your name again?'

'Sallow. I will drain the life from you. I will lay my hands upon you and you shall know the true meaning of fear.'

'Right. So how much talc do you go through each day putting that creaking onesie on?'

Sallow snarled and turned to me, one hand raised, ready to touch it to my skin.

'Try it,' I said, a knife already pressing into his side.

Alan lifted his pad: *Stop fighting. It is annoying.*

Sallow grimaced and lowered his hand, turning away from me as I put my knife away. 'Sorry, Dad.'

Behave.

A blanket of awkward silence flopped over us for the rest of the journey.

After an excruciating, half-hour drive north of Brighton and into the adjacent countryside, we arrived at our destination. A destination which, if you didn't know any better, appeared to be empty of anything even close to a building. As far as the eye could see there were only fields, grazing cows, and distant hills.

'Christ, I hate cows,' said Kirklander, keeping his distance from a couple of the mindless beasts chewing the cud.

'I, Sallow, also do not like cows.'

'You two have so much in common, you should hang out,' I said, following after Alan as he strode across the field, the cows ignoring us.

'Sallow does not hang out.'

'Hey, I wasn't offering, whitey,' replied Kirklander.

The Upside-Down Tower is a prison for powerful Uncanny people. It's called the Upside-Down Tower as it doesn't stretch into the sky, instead it stretches down, deep into the earth, like a tick burrowing into the planet's flesh. And it was, well, upside-down. Some say a giant tore it from its foundations a thousand years ago and plunged it into the ground like a dagger. Which sounds kinda cool but I'm pretty sure, rather than burrowing into the ground, that would have just completely destroyed the building.

Cool image though, eh?

Now you don't leave something like that out in the open for any old Tom, Dick, or cow to stumble over. The tower needed to be hidden, protected, secret, and so the building existed in a gap between two realms. A smudge between this reality and another.

Alan held up his pad: *Wait*.

'Have I stood in a cow pat?' asked Kirklander, showing me the bottom of one boot.

Alan placed his hands against the air, as though he was a mime pretending he was trapped inside an invisible box. His hands began to glow bright red, sweat appearing on top of his bald head and racing down his skin as he dug his fingers into the air. There was a sound like fingernails on a chalkboard, then Alan pulled open a tear in reality; a glowing, white void.

Follow.

He stepped into the pulsating white opening and the three of us followed, the tear closing as Sallow stepped through last.

We found ourselves in a blur of a world, our surroundings a painting someone had spilled water over. The only clear thing, the only thing with sharp, defined lines and colours, was the one storey above-ground section of the tower. An uninspiring-looking, windowless hump built of dull, grey bricks. A solid wooden door with a peephole set at knee-level was the only way in and out. Alan gave the door a bash with one of his meaty fists and the peephole slid back.

'State your name.'

Alan crouched and fed his pad through the peephole. The pad was passed back a few seconds later and the sound of multiple metal bolts being scraped back made me squirm and clench my teeth. The door creaked open to reveal a small creature that looked like Yoda had impregnated a frog. This was Loka, the Upside-Down Tower's front of house guy. Loka smelled even worse than he looked, an odour like feet mixed with morning breath.

'Alan,' said Loka with a nod. Alan waved.

'Been a while, Loka,' I said, trying not to breathe through my nose.

'I thought you were in prison?'

'They let me out for bad behaviour.'

'A joke?'

'Yup..'

Loka frowned and nodded. 'Not a very good one.'

'Everyone's a critic.'

Loka pointed the spear he was holding at myself, Kirklander, and Sallow. 'No weapons inside my tower, drop them on the ground before you enter or I'll stick my spear in your belly.'

'Is charm a weapon?' asked Kirklander, winking at me.

'Not in your case,' replied Loka.

'Ooh, burn,' I said, dropping three knives of various sizes to the dirt, as Kirklander and Sallow similarly relieved themselves of anything shooty, blasty, or stabby.

'All right, come on in then,' said Loka, turning and waving us on.

The door led into a single, large space. The waiting room. If you want to picture the general ambience of the place, imagine a castle dungeon at midnight. There were no windows for outside light, no light fixtures. The space was lit by a few, fat candles dotted around the place in iron candle holders fixed to the dark, damp bricks of the walls. Just enough candles to cut through the gloom, but not enough to properly illuminate the place. They seemed to like the bleak vibe they had going on.

A second door—metal this time, the door that led down to the numerous sub-levels of the tower—stood on the far wall. Apart from that, the space had a desk and chair that Loka settled himself behind, and a few other chairs scattered around for those of us waiting. There was no table with ancient magazines piled on top to help visitors kill time, even though I'd suggested it on more than one occasion.

'Now you wait for the guard,' said Loka. 'The guard will take you when ready.'

Alan settled onto a chair near the entrance as we three assassins paced up and down the waiting room floor, waiting our turn. Actually, we were stood on the waiting room ceiling. Because of the upside-down thing.

Nobody knew quite how long the Upside-Down Tower had existed. Some say it's always been here, which, again, makes very little sense to me, but these are the sort of things Uncanny people like to say to each other. Bit tiresome.

'Sallow,' came a booming voice as one of the tower's jailers stepped into the reception, a seven-foot woman in grey overalls, a flaming torch in one hand, a spear in the other.

'I am Sallow,' he replied.

'Why does that pasty prick get seen first?' I asked, hands on my hips.

Settle down.

I turned from Alan and crossed my arms, sulking, as Sallow crossed the reception area to join the jailer.

It had been explained that we would each be given five minutes to speak to the prisoner. To ask questions about the witnesses. Anything they might know that would help. By law, Jenkins & Jenkins couldn't give us any information, we had to find it all for ourselves. This was the first step down that road.

'I wonder who the prisoner is,' said Kirklander, sidling up to me.

'I'm not talking to you, still, you dick.'

Kirklander nodded and twirled his magical staff.

'You got it fixed then?' I said.

'After you broke it over my skull? Yeah. I got it fixed. My head still hurts sometimes though.'

'Carry on talking and the rest of you will hurt too.'

To say me and Kirklander had a complicated history was an understatement. An understatement that included lots of very good sex, lots of very good fights, and lots of not very good double-crossings that had, on one occasion, landed me in jail. Most recently he'd tried to muscle in on a job I was doing for a demon that had ended with me beating the ever-living crap out of him and stealing his car. Which, I'm not going to lie, felt *really bloody good*.

'I take it you're still angry at me, then?' he said.

'Just assume I'm always angry at you, it'll save time.'

Kirklander laughed and ran his hand through his long, dark hair. I tried to ignore the flutter in my chest. And the one in my knickers. Stupid, sexy, Kirklander.

'You shouldn't trust Sallow, by the way,' he said.

'I don't trust either one of you.'

'Hey, at least when I double-cross I do it with charm and a twinkle.'

I considered breaking his staff over his skull a second time, though, if I'm being honest, I was also considering getting my mitts on his, uh, *other* staff. If you know what I mean. Was that too subtle?

I mean his penis.

'Sallow is a piece of shit,' said Kirklander.

'Aren't we all? And by we, I mean you.'

Kirklander grinned and raised his hands. 'Hey, fine. I'm just trying to be a friend. Give you a little warning about the person we've found ourselves in bed with.'

'There is no bed.'

'Maybe not today,' he replied with a wink, 'but you know we'll get back there eventually.'

I shot him a cold, hard stare. 'Listen to me very carefully. We're not friends. We're not colleagues. We're definitely not lovers. I don't need your advice. I don't need your help. I don't need your... uh... your anything. At all. So just stay away from me and let me do my job.'

Twenty minutes later Sallow returned with the guard and it was my turn to see the client.

I was led down stone corridors and musty, winding staircases, rats scuttling away into the black as our feet disturbed them. Past door after door, cell after cell, prisoner after prisoner. Cries, screams, and sobs echoed up and down the tower as thousands of prisoners raged and catcalled. The deeper down, down, down into the tower, into the earth, I was led, the more oppressive the atmosphere became. The concentrated pressure of hate, of anguish, of evil weighing down on my soul. I did my best not to actually touch the large, dark, damp blocks of stone that made up the walls. Some animal part of my brain feared that the pain and anger from the centuries it had spent housing the very worst of the Uncanny Kingdom might infect me.

I had enough pain and anger of my own.

'Here,' said the guard, pointing at a wooden door that looked identical to the many, many wooden doors we'd already passed.

There didn't seem to be any way to differentiate between

cells, no numbers, no names on them. Christ alone knew how the guards kept it all in their heads.

My escort pressed a palm to the door and the locking mechanism responded. I heard a metal *clunk* as it unlocked.

'Neat trick,' I remarked, 'can you teach me that? I'm always losing my keys.'

'You have five minutes,' responded the guard.

I pushed open the door. The room inside was gloomy, lit by a single lamp, the first electronic device I'd seen inside. The floor was stone and covered in straw.

I readied my body, firing up my tattoos and preparing to pull in some extra strength in case I needed to defend myself.

'Hello,' came the voice of the cell's occupant.

'Howdy,' I replied.

The prisoner was a woman, sat, legs crossed, relaxed, on a neatly made bunk. The only other furniture in the room was a stool and a small table.

'You must be Erin Banks,' said the woman.

'I suppose I must be,' I replied, edging around the cell, keeping my distance from her. Now, I'm a tough bastard, but there was something about the energy this woman gave off, the relaxed confidence that she was in control despite being trapped like a pig in a pen. It put me right on edge. Brought me out in gooseflesh all over.

'My name is Liyta,' said the woman, 'it is so very good to meet you.'

The name tickled the back of my brain. I'd heard it before, I was sure of it, but I couldn't remember how or why.

Liyta looked to be in her early forties, with jet black hair cut into a severe flapper girl bob. Her eyes, a bright green shining out even in the gloom of the cell, stayed on me, on my face, never once looking away, barely even blinking. Her slim, delicate hands rested calmly upon her thighs. She wore the simple, grey jumpsuit that all of those held captive in the Upside-Down Tower wore, though somehow on her it looked stylish.

'Is it a nice day outside, Erin Banks?'

'It's all right,' I replied, not really wanting to get into a conversation with the woman. I was there for information, not chit-chat.

'The people who are going to testify against you. Tell me about them.'

Liyta smiled and it made my stomach twist. There was something... wrong with it. Like the smile was a lie that hid bad, bad things.

'Look upon the table to your left. Three pictures. Those are for you.'

I glanced towards the table, making sure to keep Liyta in my field of vision. She wasn't tied to the bunk, wasn't bolted to the wall, wasn't shackled in any way. I needed to be careful. Something told me that letting my guard down in front of this woman would be a very bad idea, unless I liked the idea of a set of teeth chowing down on my windpipe.

There was a thin, cardboard folder on the table. I picked it up and opened it. Inside were three pictures.

'Tell me about these people,' I said.

'Do you know who I am?' asked Liyta.

'Don't know, don't care. Tell me about the witnesses.'

'As you wish. The first one is named Marie Lendle.'

The picture showed a woman in her late teens with blonde hair and an easy smile. Her whole life ahead of her and I was going to do all I could do to put an end to it. If you hadn't realised by now that I wasn't an altogether good person, then I'm sorry if I'm bursting your bubble here. I'm a killer. A murderer for hire. It doesn't matter to me who the person I'm paid to take care of is, it's my job.

And I enjoy it.

'She might look young. Look delicate. But Marie Lendle is a shifter.'

'What does she shift into?'

'Something rather marvellous with large claws and oodles of teeth.'

I turned to the second picture. A man in his fifties.

'Why are you helping me?' asked Liyta.

'Money. What's this guy's name?'

'Jarvis Fuller. Do you know why I'm locked up, Erin Banks?'

'Doesn't matter. None of my business. Killing people, that's my business.'

Liyta laughed and I found myself taking a step back as a chill flushed over my skin.

'I have a lot of time in here to play among my memories. Just this morning I was recalling the time I convinced a girl to kill herself. She was thirteen years old, not nearly old enough to be carrying any real pain, but I found it in her. A few well placed words and the girl was no more. Her parents cried and cried and cried. I thought it a very good day's work.'

She was trying to get a reaction out of me. Maybe this woman wasn't anything special after all. Maybe she was just another run-of-the-mill mental trying to push my buttons. Trying to make me scared and put me on the back foot.

'Look, I don't care who you are or what you do for kicks. I'm here to do a job and get paid, that's it, so you can save your *ooh, scary stories* for somebody who gives a shit, right?'

Liyta tilted her head to one side, ever so slightly, her eyes not leaving mine. 'Jarvis Fuller is a low-level wizard, on his mother's side.'

'What kind of magic can he pull off?'

'You lost someone.'

My heart skipped a beat.

'Shut up.'

Liyta smiled.

Cursing my hand as it trembled ever so slightly, I turned to the third picture.

The third picture was very bad news.

'That's a demon. That's a fucking demon.'

Well, awesome. A shifter and a low-level wizard were one thing, but a demon? That was practically a suicide mission.

'Gjindor is a minor demon. He can be stopped.'

'Easy for you to say,' I replied as I looked again at the picture of a shabby, sore covered man with thin, greasy hair plastered to his corpse flesh..

'A brother.'

'What?'

'Your brother was taken.'

My chest tightened as Liyta's green eyes glittered in the dark.

'Who told you that?'

'You did,' replied Liyta, rising slowly to her feet. For the first time, I realised how tall she was. Six foot at least.

'Stay where you are, bitch.'

'So much anger in you. You are full of the dark, Erin Banks. So much delicious pain. Such loss. Such *fear*. What was his name?'

My back was pressed against the damp cool of the cell wall, my fists two wrecking balls. How could she know about my brother? Someone must have told her.

Liyta took a single step forward.

'Stay where you are!' I demanded, heading for the door, folder of pictures tucked under my arm.

'I want to thank you for helping me, Erin Banks.'

'You can get to fuck,' I replied, my head a whirl of confusion, my fist banging on the door so the guard would open up.

Liyta remained still, and for a moment it was as though I could see my brother, floating in a ball of red magic, hovering somewhere between us.

The door opened and I stepped out into the corridor outside, gasping for air. How long had I been holding my breath?

'Enjoy your stay in there, fuck-face,' I said, my heart beating like a jackhammer.

'His name is James,' said Liyta as the door closed on her and the lock clunked into place.

5

I think we can all agree that was all a bit unnerving.

I hadn't bothered waiting for Kirklander to get done and for Alan to drop us back. Instead, I got out of that sunken place and into the fresh air as fast as I could, and phoned for a taxi to take me home. Kirklander had asked me what was up, as if he actually cared, but I'd shoved him aside and headed for the door. The last thing I wanted was for him to see me looking upset. Looking weak.

That woman didn't know shit about James, not really. All she knew were the things I knew, things she'd sensed in me, stolen from my mind. It was only when I stepped out of her cell and followed the guard back to the surface that I realised she'd been inside my head. It was only once I removed myself from her presence that I felt Liyta's finger-prints, felt the grazes she'd left as she rummaged around in there, looking for bad stuff she could use against me. She didn't know anything about my brother, all she had was parlour tricks, and I wasn't falling for them.

And yet, that woman had scared the ever-living shit out of me.

As the taxi drove me home I opened the folder, tipped out the three photos I'd been given, and concentrated on the witnesses I'd been hired to terminate. Focused on their faces, on the little bits of information Liyta had given me. That bitch had tried toying with me, tried to make me feel like crap, but that was over with. I wouldn't be seeing her again. What I would be seeing was my bank balance getting a few more zeroes as soon as I took care of the fuckers in the photos sitting on my lap.

Of course, there was more than one hurdle to overcome before that happened.

First of all, I had Kirklander and Sallow racing to beat me to each of the three witnesses. The terms of this sort of contract were clear: to claim their fee, a contracted assassin had to return to the office of their employer—in this case, Jenkins & Jenkins—with the eyeball of a deceased witness. Because there were multiple witnesses, there was a single pot of money, and said assassin—that would be me—got a slice of it for each eyeball returned. Three witnesses, three eyeballs, three chunks of the bounty. It was a race, a competition. Best case scenario, I beat those tits to all three witnesses and claimed all three chunks. Worst case scenario, I ran around putting myself in danger for the next few days and failed to claim a single eyeball or any of the cash.

That would really be something of a bummer.

The other problem was just who it was I was being paid to kill. Now, the first two would no doubt cause me trouble; the shifter and the wizard. It didn't matter how low-level they might be, anyone with access to that sort of magic was capable of being dangerous. Capable of leaving me dead in a gutter somewhere. But they weren't the real cause for concern. That honour went to witness numero three.

Gjindor.

A bloody, bastarding demon.

If this had been a demon like the Tall Man, a fully fledged, super-powerful demon of the High Order, then I wouldn't even be considering it. I'd take my chances going for the first two bits of the bounty and leave that big boy to the other two. But Liyta had said he was a minor demon. How minor I didn't know, but it was something to look into. Minor or not, it was going to be a very foolish thing for me to attempt. Even an all-mighty wizard like Giles L'Merrier takes a calming breath or two before facing off with a demon, and I was very far down the ladder compared to that egg-headed magic man. All I had were tattoos that upped my strength, my reflexes, my speed, and helped me put myself back together after I'd taken a beating. If I tried to go up against even a minor demon I'd probably end up looking like a fly who picked a fight with the windshield of a speeding car.

Still, I do like a challenge.

A demon though. Bit weird. Why would a demon be standing as a witness in a trial? Justice was not exactly high on their to-do lists. A demon with a conscience, maybe? That didn't sound likely.

As the taxi dropped me off and I plodded down the alleyway to my flat, I found myself surprised I was even considering it. Considering taking on a demon. Was I that egotistical? (yes). Was I that desperate for danger, for distraction? (again, a big fat yo).

I walked by a sideboard stacked high with overdue bills and into my sparsely furnished lounge, where I belly-flopped onto the sofa. My phone buzzed my pocket. I groaned, rolled over onto my back, and pulled it out. There was a text from Lana: *She's still unconscious. Are you going to visit? Please call me.*

I tossed my phone aside and looked again at the picture of Gjindor. Yeah, I needed the danger and distraction. But I wasn't completely mad, I'd leave that sucker for last, as I'm sure both Sallow and Kirklander would, too.

I reached for my phone again and re-read Lana's message, even considered replying.

'Fuck!' I yelled, annoyed. This was stupid, I had a job to do. Money to earn. People to kill. Competitors to beat.

The chase was on and I was lying on my couch, sulking.

I ignored Lana and fired off a message to someone who could help me: *Oi, Cupid, get your chubby arse over to the pier, one hour.*

I stood, took a deep breath, and smiled. Danger, here I come.

'Who else is on the case, then?' asked Parker as I pulled back the curtain of his tattoo parlour and sunk into his leather couch.

'So you knew there'd be others?'

'Course, girl. Jenkins boys said the time-frame was tight, makes sense to go out heavy.'

'Well, thanks for the heads up, you arse.'

'You're a petulant bitch, you know that?'

I laughed, then winced, my body aching. I reached into my leather jacket and pulled out a couple of pills and a hip flask, which, on that day, was full of a particularly cheap and nasty whisky. I swallowed the pills, chased them down with the whisky, and felt my body relax.

'How's your bones, girl?'

'Still on the inside, thanks.'

'Best place for them, I say. So, who else?'

'Sallow and Kirklander.'

Parker drew a breath noisily between his clenched teeth. 'Sallow bad news.'

'He's a pasty turd who dresses like a horror cosplayer.'

'He's a turd, but he bad, too. Greedy. Don't turn your back on him.'

Like I had anything to be worried about from that guy, Parker could be such a worrier.

'Did you know Kirklander was gonna be there?'

'Course not. I would've told my girl if her fave was in the game.'

'Fave? Do fuck off.'

Parker threw his head back and laughed, his short dreadlocks dancing around like they had a life of their own.

My phone buzzed and I pulled it out, expecting a little emotional blackmail from my cousin. Instead, I saw Kirklander's name. *Oof, so she's a fun piece of work, hey? Call me.*

I grimaced and deleted the message.

'Talk of the devil?' grinned Parker, then threw his head back again, far enough that I could see his gold fillings.

'Fuck you, Parks,' I replied, but found myself smiling anyway.

I often wondered what it was about Kirklander that stopped me from keeping him in the past, even after everything he'd done to me. Yeah, he was beautiful, and dynamite in the sack, but that wasn't enough to give him a pass, right? Was I really that shade of cliché that couldn't do without the emotionally unavailable bad boy? The piece of crap who'd do me wrong, but also do me so, so right?

Christ.

I really hate me.

'Who's the perp, then?' asked Parker as I pulled out my hip flask and took another soothing swig.

'Oh, she's a real arsehole,' I replied, 'she's called Liyta.'

Parker frowned, his brow furrowing as he sat forward.

'What you say?'

'Liyta. Why, what? What is it?'

'Damn, don't you read the news?'

'No, I'm cool, I don't read newspapers.'

'Foolish thing.'

'All right, Parks, enough with the sweet talk.'

'Liyta is bad, bad news.'

'So am I. So are most of the people we deal with. Come to think of it, so are *you*.'

'No girl, we bad, but we ain't *bad*.'

I thought about my encounter with Liyta. The things she'd said, the way I'd felt in her company. I had to admit it, I'd felt more at ease facing the Long Man, an actual, fully-fledged beast from Hell, than I had speaking to Liyta for five minutes.

'Okay, she's not going to make it on to my Christmas card list, but a job's a job, and she deserves due process as much as anyone, right?'

'Maybe,' said Parker. 'You know what they caught her for?'

'Did she drown a bag of babies?'

'Dark, girl. But no, worse. Much, much worse. Maybe this is a case we take a pass on.'

'What?' I couldn't believe what I was hearing. This was Parker's world, his job. He'd pitted me against every low-life piece of scum going, and now he was having second thoughts about a woman locked up in a prison cell?

'I need this job.'

'It's only money, girl.'

I didn't tell him the other reason. That I needed the distraction otherwise I was going to drive myself mad.

'I'm in it now. I signed the contract.'

'Some people you shouldn't help.'

'I helped a demon claim the soul of a man with a young daughter just a few weeks ago.'

Parker frowned. 'Fine. But just know I warned you.'

'I heard you loud and clear, boss.'

'This sort of thing. Helping these sort of people. It comes at a cost.'

'Lucky for us we're about to earn so much cash that we can pay that bill twice over.' I wondered how obvious my shit-eating grin was to the sightless Parker.

'Quit that shit-eating grin, girl.'

Very obvious, then.

6

Thirty minutes later I was sat on Brighton Pier, watching the seagulls circle and squawk in the night sky as I waited for Cupid to check in.

What Parker said back at the parlour had me thinking about what I did for a living. Fact was, I worked for whoever was willing to cough up the cash. Could be a demon who wanted a soul, could be an innocent who'd been wronged and needed help. Good intentions or bad, it was all the same to me. I didn't care if you'd been hurt by a bad man, I cared about getting paid. I cared about throwing my fists at people. I wasn't prejudiced, I was an equal opportunities killer, and in a way, didn't that make me one of the good guys?

This case was no different. Liyta was no different. In fact, this time I was working on behalf of the local justice system, which made this job about as kosher as it got, regardless of who it was on behalf of. Jesus, how many more people did I have to murder before I entirely stomped out that tickle of conscience at the back of my skull?

'Watch out below!' yelled a gruff voice from above.

I looked up to see a fat, awful-looking baby in a nappy hurtling down at me. 'Holy shit!' I threw myself from the bench and landed in a heap as Cupid crashed into the spot where I'd just been sat. 'What the fuck, Cupes?'

The little chubster sat up, his sausage legs dangling from the bench. He shook his wings like a dog drying itself, sending feathers flying every which way. 'All right, love?' he said before letting rip with a real paint-stripper of a burp.

'Are you drunk?'

'Sometimes.'

'Right now?'

'Oh, definitely, yeah. Pissed out of my nut.'

'You're on the clock, you little turd.'

'Oi, fucking, you know, language, young lady.'

Cupid could be a bit of a pain in the arse, but he never let me down on a job. Well, sometimes he let me down. Actually, it was pretty much a 50/50 shot whether or not he let me down, but he was cheap and my only option, so...

I stood up from the pier boardwalk and made a show of dusting myself down, not that Cupid noticed. I think he'd already forgotten his drunken, high-speed entrance. I stood over him while he toyed with his bow. A drunk baby in charge of a bow and arrows, what could possibly go wrong?

'What've you got for me?' I asked.

Cupid hugged his bow protectively. 'This is mine. I made this with me own two hands, you get your own!'

I mentioned the pain in the arse factor, yes?

I clapped my hands together, 'Focus, you little turd. Information on the Liyta case, what have you got for me?'

'No, no, cash first, information... uh... first?'

I sighed and pulled out two twenties. He grabbed them with his dirty little fist and gave them a sniff. 'Yup, that'll do.' He pushed the money into his filthy nappy and pulled something out in return. A sheet of paper with a name and address written on it.

'Here you go, then.'

I took the piece of paper, trying not to think about where he'd just pulled it from.

Harry Smith, 32 Goldhawk Drive.

'Who's this?'

'Lead prosecutor. He's the one trying to take yer evil bitch girl down.'

'Nice. Good work, baby-man.'

There are lots of rules about this sort of gig, one of which is that my employer isn't allowed to inform me who we're up against. Do that and the case gets dismissed, and by "dismissed" I mean the employer—and me—get our heads chopped off and bunged on a row of spikes outside the Uncanny Court. No trial, just plain old medieval justice. Needless to say, it pays to do things by the book.

I read the only other thing on the note...

Oli-kathru-samulty.

'What's with the gibberish?' I asked.

'Password.'

'Oh, right, right, cool.'

Lawyers in the Uncanny world tended to go a few steps beyond the standard locks and alarms when it came to protecting their homes, mainly to stop folks like me from knocking at the door. Most lawyers used magic to secure their properties. Strong magic. The kind of magic that would shred anyone who made the mistake of crossing the threshold without speaking the correct string of words first.

'You're sure that'll get me in, right? Only I like my body as it currently is, by which I mean not dead.'

Okay, maybe my ankles were a little fatter than I'd have liked, but they didn't deserve shredding.

'I'm sure, got a good source. Well, seventy percent sure, but that's a big old number.'

Great.

'Got anything on where the witnesses might be yet?' I asked.

'Never enough for you, is it?'

'Cupid...'

'I fetch you that tasty little morsel at a moment's notice and I barely get a thanks for it!'

'I'm sorry, you sensitive little dick. Thanks for the information, now please flutter away and find out some more. Please. Now.'

Cupid frowned and pushed himself up on to his fat legs so he was stood up on the bench. He slung his bow over one shoulder and hoisted his nappy up over his pot belly.

'Fine. But it'll be fifty quid a go for any witness I find.'

'Fifty! Thirty.'

'Fifty,' he insisted.

'Forty.'

'Thirty. No! Fifty!'

'Fuck it. Fine. Fifty.'

Cupid did a little dance of celebration, lost his footing, and toppled off the edge of the pier.

'You know, it might be an idea not to be pissed out of your brain on the job,' I said, leaning over the railing and shouting down at the sea.

'Fine talk coming from you,' he said, emerging from the water like a wet cat and flapping his wings until he was level with me again. 'Anyway, not my fault, I was already drunk when you messaged me. I don't wait, breath held, at your beck and call y'know. I've got a bloody life!'

With a plump middle finger by way of goodbye, Cupid's wings began to buzz and he made his way up and away. I looked again at the name and the address he'd given me. A four minute drive. Time to get to work.

G oldhawk Drive was one of the more well-to-do areas of Brighton, full of lawyers, doctors, and other rich bastards. Someone like me would stand out a mile pulling up there, but thanks to the Porsche I'd liberated from Kirklander, I fit right in.

Number 32, the home of Harry Smith, was a large, detached, mock-Victorian place. A high wall and gate kept the scum out, and through the wrought iron gate I could see a paved driveway that held three sleek, expensive cars. Light glowed from behind the closed curtains of the house.

I snapped a twig from a nearby tree and poked it through the bars of the gate. Colours rippled as the bubble of magical protection covering the property reacted to the intrusion, turning the stick into ash. Strong stuff. Pity any curious cat that might decide to take a sniff around the grounds.

I pulled out the piece of paper Cupid had given me and gave the password a squint. I wasn't a magician, and I wasn't that well-versed in how to pronounce words of power, but I was going to have to do my best, otherwise Harry Smith would stay inside and I'd stay out here.

'Oli-kathru-samulty,' I said, boldly.

I snapped off a fresh stick and poked it through the gate. The bubble rippled, reds, greens, and purples washing around the stick. A stick which did not turn to ash. Looked like I'd passed my Magic Oral test. I spoke the words out loud once more for good luck and then, with a quick look over both shoulders to make sure no one had eyes on me, I lept high, grasping the top of the gate and swinging myself up and over. I landed in a perfect three-point crouch on the driveway, my tattoos glowing from the boost they'd given me.

'Good work, Cupid,' I muttered to myself, and made a mental note to give the little turd a bonus for the good intel. I then made a second mental note to ignore the first mental note. I paid the little fucker enough as it was.

Another look around then, staying low, I darted to the house and made my way round one side. As I passed a window I heard the burble of voices inside. It sounded like children.

Just what I needed.

I found my way to a back door and pulled out my lock-picking kit. The door swung open less than ten seconds later, and I slipped inside, eyes alert, heart slow and steady. I'd broken into enough places over the years not to get panicked about it. To me, this was like heading down to the stationary cupboard to collect some new toner for the office printer. Routine. Ordinary.

That's not to say I wasn't alert to danger: mentally clocking escape routes, assessing any potential threats, considering places where people might be crouched with weapons, ready to try and take me down. I crept, I listened, I hid. Within a minute I'd managed to work out that there were three people in the house: a woman and two young kids.

Which meant no Harry Smith, unless he was holed up nice and quiet and out of sight. But this was his house, his family, so time to lean on them to find out where Harry Smith might be.

I slowly pushed the already open living room door to get a better view of what was beyond it.

The room was a little garish, like a person with no style's idea of a fancy decor. Purple carpet, purple, shiny wallpaper, a little chandelier complete with purple faux-crystals. Basically a shit-ton of purple. Prince would've loved this place. The wife was sat on the couch, her back to me. She was flicking through some trashy celebrity magazine, licking her fingers before she turned each page.

Gross.

She didn't look like she'd be much trouble.

Sat cross-legged on the floor in front of the TV were the two kids, a boy and a girl. The boy looked around six years old, the girl a year or two younger. No threat there.

I stepped into the room and closed the door behind me, cutting off the exit.

For a few seconds I stood quietly, watching the episode of *Friends* they were glued to. It was the one with Rachel's baby shower, which might also be the name of the episode. Not sure.

Time to ask some questions. I coughed politely to get their attention. It did not get their attention.

'Oi, housebreaker here!'

That did it.

They all twisted as one, the wife giving off a little yelp of surprise.

'Who are you? How did you get in my house?'

'Okay, no, I'll be the one asking the questions, all right? First off, what's your name?'

The woman had her magazine balled in her fists, pressed to her chest.

'Come on, I can't just keep calling you "the wife". I mean, what is this, the Fifties?'

'Carol. My name is Carol.'

'There we go. Not so hard, is it?'

Carol rose to her feet. She was slim. Rich bitch slim. Her hair was expensively dyed a lush, dark blonde, and she was wearing a leopard skin patterned silk blouse that was open enough to show off a good acre of chest.

'Mummy...' said the little girl.

'It's okay, honey. Everything's okay,' said Carol, holding out an arm for the girl to cling to. The boy needed no such reassurance, instead he stood glaring at me defiantly. Tough little dude.

'Cute kids,' I said.

'Don't talk about them,' replied Carol, snarling.

'Ooh, good feisty MILF energy, Carol. I like it.'

I pulled out my knife, all nonchalant, and patted the blade against the flank of my leg. 'Where's your hubby, Carol, I want to ask him a thing or two.'

Carol didn't answer.

'Carol...'

'He's not here, go away!' said the young boy.

'Wish I could, but this is my job. Your mum understands, right?'

Carol sighed and sagged. 'Look, he's not in, and I don't know anything about any cases he works on.'

'You're sure he's not upstairs, hunting around the lock box he keeps his twelve-gauge in?'

'He went out for a run,' said Carol.

'Pff... okay. I guess we're all waiting here until he gets back then. Take a seat. All of you.'

I pointed at the couch and Carol and her daughter sat, keeping their eyes on me.

'You too, tough guy,' I told the boy.

'Come here to Mummy,' said Carol, reaching out to him.

The boy grimaced at me, then joined his mum and sister on the couch.

I leaned against the wall by the door, waiting. 'You know,' I said, 'this episode is okay, but it's not a patch on the earlier seasons, right?'

They didn't answer.

But I was right.

It took thirty awkward minutes before the front door open and closed.

'Carol, I'm back. I saw a right oddball a few streets over. He was...' Harry's words trailed away as he stepped into the living room to be greeted by his terrified-looking wife. 'What's wrong?'

I pressed the point of my dagger into his back. 'One false move and I'm gonna do something very painful to you, Harry.'

He flinched but didn't try to move away. He was breathing heavily, his shorts and t-shirt a little damp with sweat, but I couldn't tell if that was through fear or the run he'd just returned from.

'You do realise the filth you're helping, I take it?' asked Harry.

'Oh, Jesus, has Parker been bending your ear, too? Get over there.' I prodded him forward with the knife and he rounded the couch to join Carol and the kids.

'How is she in here, Harry? You promised that wizard was good.'

'He was. He is! Best money can buy.'

Carol pointed at me. 'Oh, yeah, well worth the cash, you idiot.'

'In Harry's defence,' I said, 'every protection spell has a lock that can be picked.'

Carol rounded on her husband. 'You never told me that!'

'Because if I had you'd have shouted at me about the stupid, dangerous job I have.'

'Oh, Harry, secrets between couples never end well, trust me,' I said.

'Daddy, I'm scared,' cried the little girl.

'Don't worry, she's not going to hurt us. Is she?'

I frowned, tossed the knife handle-over-blade into the air, and caught it. 'Maybe, maybe not, depends if you tell me what I want to hear.'

'Look, fair enough, you found me, you get your reward, congratulations.'

'Where are the witnesses?'

'I only know where Marie Lendle is holed up.'

Marie Lendle, the shifter.

'You wouldn't be lying to me now, would you Harry? I'd hate to make you piss blood in front of your kids.'

The little girl whimpered and clung tighter to her parents.

'It makes no sense for one of us to know all the locations. Think it through.'

Yeah, that tracked. If someone knew all the locations then it'd make my job way too easy. This way there was a chance one or more witnesses would make it through the trial alive.

'Okay, Marie Lendle, where's she at, Harry?'

He sighed. 'It's not as easy as all that.'

'I'm sorry, maybe it'll get easier if I punch Carol in the neck? What do you think?'

'No! Look, I know where she is. Well, I can think of three places she might be.'

'Are you taking the piss?'

'It's like you're annoyed we don't make it easy for you. We're actually trying to get this trial to go ahead, you know.'

'All right, all right, stop your whining.'

Great. So I was going to be hauling arse all over town, and what was the betting it would be the last of the three places I visited that Marie was holed up in? Of course, there was also the strong possibility that Harry would call ahead and warn Marie to move to another safe house while I was in transit.

Then again, this wasn't my first rodeo.

'Okay, phones, now.'

With a little extra cajoling, Harry and Carol handed over their phones, which I then smashed under the heel of my boot.

'I was due an upgrade anyway,' Carol sulked.

I pointed to the radiator and pulled out a couple of zip ties. 'Wrists.'

'Oh now, come on,' said Harry.

I gave him a dig in the ribs that left him doubled-over, gasping for air. 'Pretty please.'

'On second thoughts... great idea,' he said.

I tied them to the radiator, and then the two kids for good measure.

Okay, no one was getting the word out before I made my rounds.

'Addresses, now.'

Harry did as asked.

'And that's the truth, right? Only I'll be very upset with your wife, very upset with your kids, if you've just fed me some hot bullshit.'

'It's the truth.'

I held his gaze but he didn't look away. 'Thanks, Harry.

Beautiful family you have, we should do this again sometime soon.'

'Oh, shit,' said Harry.

'Okay, we don't have to do it again.'

'The oddball,' said Harry, pointing past me. I turned sharply, knife raised, to find a figure standing in the doorway doing his best to look imposing. A figure dressed in lots of leather.

'Thank you for the information,' said Sallow.

Bollocks. Huge ones.

7

Okay, so the situation I was in had the look of something likely to go south pretty fast. I'd orchestrated a simple break-in and semi-hostage-ish situation, only for leather boy to crash the party with his fancy strength-sapping powers and glam metal kecks.

My tattoos glowed crimson as they soaked in the Uncanny charge from the air around me, pumping me up, getting me ready for a ruckus. To be honest, I was kinda hoping it would come to this. I'd been wanting to cave that arsehole's skull in from the day we met.

'Have you been following me, you creepy creep?'

'I am Sallow, I do not follow.'

'But the creepy creep part was spot-on, right?'

Sallow snarled at me, one hand raised, ready to touch me if I tried to get any closer. I aimed my knife his way. 'Easy there, emo, I'll have the business end of this in your nuts before you can blink.'

'I take it you two are after the same thing?' Harry interjected.

'Make that three of us,' came a third voice as Kirklander stepped into the room.

'Well this is a clusterfuck,' I said.

I was annoyed, sure, but more than that, stood in front of Harry and his family, I felt embarrassed. This was a legit case and we were supposed to be professionals. Instead, here we were, tumbling one by one into the prosecutor's house, stepping on each other's toes.

'So that's three strangers that have managed to bypass that protection spell you paid for,' said Carol, eyes glaring accusingly at her husband. 'I don't suppose that wizard sold some magic beans too, did he?'

Harry sighed and pinched the bridge of his nose. 'Can we get this over with? I think my wife is eager to yell at me.'

'Women, am I right, Harry?' said Kirklander.

'Look, do you need me to repeat the locations or did you all hear them?'

'I, Sallow, heard you.'

'Got 'em, boss,' said Kirklander.

'Can we talk? Outside,' I said, and stalked out of the room, Sallow and Kirklander in tow.

We left the prosecutor's property, across the drive and on to the pavement outside.

'Okay, so we've got to work out what to do next,' I said.

'How do you mean?' asked Kirklander.

'Look, that shit-show in there made us all look like idiots. Fair enough, you are an idiot, and Sallow is at least three steps below that, but I like to get things done right. Right?'

'Baby, I love it when you get mean.'

I ignored that.

'There are three possible locations and three of us. How about rather than all trying to sprint to the same place we take one each? After that, it's a free-for-all. Make sense?'

'I, Sallow, do not take orders from a normal such as you.'

'Hey,' said Kirklander, raising his staff, 'watch your mouth.'

'I can fight my own battles, thanks.' Yes, a little bit of me got all butterflies-in-the-stomach when Kirk stood up for me, but that part could sod right off.

'This is the easiest way to go, all right? Or are we all going to run to the same place and see who wins like a bunch of little kids at a three-legged race?'

Sallow frowned. 'I, Sallow, have decided that we should choose one address each.'

'What a great idea, Swallow,' I replied.

'*Sallow.*'

'Ha,' said Kirklander, 'Swallow.'

'Do not test me, insects. I am Sallow. All who face me end up on their knees, screaming. Screaming as the dark of everlasting nothing comes to claim them.'

'How many times did you rehearse that line in the mirror?' asked Kirklander. 'And it still doesn't make sense.'

Sallow took his address and left.

'I thought he'd never bugger off,' said Kirklander, leaning on his staff.

'The second address is yours. Go away.'

I turned to leave, only to find a hand on my forearm. I spun and kicked the staff from under him, causing Kirklander to stagger, arms windmilling, before he righted himself.

'Nice,' he said, retrieving his staff. 'Can we talk, like adults for a second?'

'I'm not sure you can do that for even that long.'

'Ah, funny. Nice one. Look, we've obviously got a problem here.'

I opened my mouth to yell various things at him, only for Kirklander to step back, hands raised.

'Whoa now, before you go into full berserker mode, I wasn't talking about our relationship.'

'Good, because that doesn't exist.'

'I have a proposition for you.'

'The answer is no.'

'One third of the bounty doesn't sound too great to me. What do you say to you and me teaming up, murdering Sallow, and splitting the entire bounty between the two of us? Sound good?'

It actually did sound really, really good. I smiled. 'Kirklander?'

'Yes, baby,' he replied, leaning in.

'Get to fuck.' I turned on my heel and headed towards the parked Porsche.

'This makes sense, you know it does!'

'I'm not interested in teaming up. Ever. Full stop!'

'I'm trying to do you a favour here!'

I stopped and turned, fury coursing through me, my tattoos livid with power. 'Say that again.'

'Fine. Every man, woman, and leather-clad pervert for themselves. Got it.'

I turned and headed for the Porsche.

The engine roared as my foot stomped on the accelerator and the car peeled away, leaving Kirklander for dust. Soon enough, Brighton receded in the rear view as I left the city, heading for pastures new.

I couldn't help but be pissed off at Kirklander for having a great idea that I couldn't bring myself to agree with. Because yes, one bounty split three ways sucked more arse than a professional arse sucker during a sold out arse-sucking festival. I had no problem with the idea of killing Sallow to up my cut. No problem whatsoever. He was a professional killer, just like me, just like Kirklander, he knew he was fair game for a knife through the rib cage. Plus, his fashion sense pretty much demanded someone gut the guy.

I let forth a long sigh as I eased off the accelerator. Chances were we'd all end up dead at some point, and in a less than natural manner. Came with the territory. But the idea of palling up with Kirklander, with trusting him again after his last betrayal... well, it didn't fill me with roses and dancing Muppets.

So fuck that.

The address I took from the prosecutor turned out to be not so much an address as a field. I parked up in a layby on the side of the road, a few miles outside of Brighton. The smell of the countryside filled my nostrils, by which I mean the place stank of shit. I zipped up my jacket and scanned my surroundings. Hills, fields, and trees as far as the eye could see. Plus one added extra. In the centre of a field of tall grass to my left was a caravan, minus a vehicle to haul it.

'Right then.'

I vaulted over the wooden fence that enclosed the field and strode towards the dilapidated caravan. I shivered as buried memories of damp English holidays from my childhood bubbled up. The three of us jammed into a tiny caravan with a toilet that flushed one time in a dozen. That was before James. Before my brother was born. We never got the chance to go on a family holiday between him coming into the world and being taken from it.

As the caravan got closer, I wondered if my mum, now laid up in a hospital bed, ever thought back to those cramped caravan trips we took, before everything went bad. I wondered if she thought about how she would carry me on her shoulders across muddy fields, the both of us laughing and singing made-up songs at the tops of our lungs, our only audience a few disinterested cows.

Did she?

What was about to happen was my own fault. I'm a professional. At least, I was supposed to be, but I certainly wasn't acting that way. I'd been given the known hiding place of a witness—a witness the prosecution knew I'd been hired to kill—and there I was, wandering into a potential trap with my head in the clouds. Too busy reminiscing. Too busy feeling sad about a past that felt like fiction now.

I didn't knock on the door. Didn't call out to anyone who might be lurking inside. Instead, I soaked the surrounding magic into my body and tore the flimsy door from its hinges without a thought for the consequences. It was only once I'd stepped into the caravan that I realised I'd made a mistake. That I hadn't been thinking straight about the situation.

As the dank innards of the caravan crept over my skin and its stench invaded my nostrils, I noticed two things. First, the caravan was empty. Marie Lendle was gone fishin'.

And then there was the second thing.

A very bad thing.

A very bad thing that—if I hadn't been busy thinking about my mum and holidays and stupid happy times—I would have been on high alert for.

The caravan was booby-trapped.

What kind of trap? Some Uncanny incantation that stripped the flesh from my bones before turning those bones to goop? A magical hex that disappeared me from reality?

Nope.

A good, old-fashioned, no-nonsense bomb. You can't beat the classics.

As I stepped into the caravan, my tattoos glowing with Uncanny power, my senses heightened, I felt my foot push down on a trigger hidden under a welcome mat. I felt the click through my foot, my ankle, heard the electrical connection spark, smelled the combustible potential about to rip through the place.

Rip through me.

I had barely a breath. Barely a heartbeat. Barely a second before the bomb went off. Body souped up by the magic I'd drawn into my tattoos, I twisted, crouched, and propelled myself out into the field outside.

And then the caravan erupted.

8

I could smell bacon. I could hear it crackling in the pan. Dad must have been cooking up breakfast on the portable stove outside. That delicious, bacony smell coiling through the cool morning air and through the open caravan door, finding its way to my nose as I slept curled up in a sleeping bag on the small, padded seat that doubled as my bed.

I used to play a game when I was little. After waking, sometimes, I'd try to pretend I was still asleep for as long as I could. I'd lay there, eyes shut tight, and listen to my parents moving around. Listen to them talking. Maybe they'd say stuff they wouldn't normally say around me when they knew I was awake. Maybe I'd hear secrets. Special secrets.

It never lasted long, I was terrible at keeping still once I'd woken up.

'Okay, you're awake,' said Mum.

'No, I'm not,' I replied.

Damn.

A pair of hands grabbed me and lifted me into the air, my sleeping bag slipping off and falling to the floor as Mum lifted me to her face and blew raspberries on my tummy. I screamed and laughed and squirmed.

She carried me outside where Dad was on his knees before the stove, bacon sizzling before him in a pool of melted butter.

'I think we should ask her,' said Dad.

'What, now?'

'Tell me!'

'She should be part of this.'

'Tell me, tell me!' I yelled.

Mum dropped me on the grass. 'Okay,' she said, grinning.

I smiled, my toes digging into the grass, my hands clenching, desperate to hear.

'We've been thinking...' said Dad.

'About what?'

'Well,' said Mum, 'we think it might be nice if the three of us became four.'

I frowned. 'What d'you mean? Like a cat?'

Mum laughed.

'No,' said Dad.

'I want a cat!'

'We were thinking more about a little brother or sister for you.'

It took another two years before James finally appeared. My little brother. But that was when I first heard about him. About the idea of him. After that came another idea. The idea that I'd be a big sister, and that I'd protect my baby brother. Protect him from anything.

I didn't always remember that conversation. Only sometimes, when I slept. When I dreamed. I wished I could go back to that moment, but that moment was long gone. No more waking up in a caravan, my parents holding hands, laughing. No more good news. No more baby brother.

The bomb would have killed me if I hadn't managed to dive away in time. It should have killed me despite that. The damage I'd taken would have slaughtered an ordinary person, but not me. My legs were shattered, the bones broken and twisted. My back was burned all over, one side of my face, too. But I was alive. In agony, but alive.

I got my breathing under control as best I could, and gritted my teeth. As the ruptured skeleton of the caravan blazed behind me, I willed some more magic into my tattoos. The sharpened reflexes the Uncanny ink had provided me with, the extra strength it gave to my legs, had enabled me to leap far enough from the explosion's epicentre to survive the blast. Now, hopefully, that same ink would be able to fix the injuries I'd sustained, before death claimed me.

The urge to vomit overwhelmed me. I twisted to one side, the movement causing pain to shoot all through my body. I half-screamed, half-threw up.

Okay.

Okay.

I couldn't let the pain overcome me. Couldn't give in. The tattoos wouldn't work unless I made them work. Unless I forced them to put this broken doll back together.

I didn't want to die.

I couldn't die.

Wouldn't give in.

Especially not through my own stupidity. Dying in a one-on-one in a fight, okay, that I could maybe come to terms with. But not like this. Not because I was distracted and dumb and sloppy.

I breathed long and slow. The pain was everywhere, but

I did my best to ignore it. I took the pain, scooped it up in my hands and placed it in a box. Then I closed the box and kicked it as far away as I could. Kicked it down a deep, dark hole.

'Come... come on...'

The magic began to seep into my charred body, and I soaked it up like a sponge. I could feel myself becoming stronger even as my grip on life grew weaker.

'Come on...'

As flames continued to eat away the remains of the caravan, I stepped further and further away from the edge. Bones knitted, flesh healed, burns vanished. I'd been far gone—almost too far gone for my tattoos to help—but over the course of the next twenty minutes I undid the damage the explosion had done me.

Finally, I sat up, exhausted, tattoos aching, my whole body drenched in sweat.

I wanted to yell out in relief. Tell Death to go fuck himself in every hole he had. But I was too relieved, and too exhausted, to do anything more than stumble away from the wreckage, back to the Porsche, and get the hell away from that place.

I didn't get far.

I'd expended too much energy, leaned on my tattoos too much, to just carry on like everything was fine. Within a few minutes I was parked up again, sunk against the headrest, fast asleep.

I t was my phone that woke me. I jerked back to consciousness. It was early, almost half-six. The morning was raw, the sunrise angry. I must have slept for hours. I grabbed my phone and checked the name.

Lana.

I should have ignored it like I had been doing, but having just had a very near-death experience, and still being a little fuggy from a deep sleep, I hit Answer.

'Yeah...?' I slurred.

'Are you drunk?'

'Unfortunately not. What do you want?'

'It's about your mum.'

I sat up, anger flashing over me. 'I don't care! How many times do we have to go over this?'

'I don't believe you.'

'If I want to know, I'll ask. You can stop playing the perfect niece, the perfect cousin!'

'Erin, what's wrong?'

'What's wrong is you! Listen, I've already fucked myself over because of her. You know how close I came to dying because of her? Because she's been on my mind when she doesn't deserve to be? Well, not again!'

'Erin...'

'Phone me when she's dead. No, actually, don't phone, I won't pick up. Text me. Bye.'

I hung up and seethed for a few seconds. If this had been a cartoon, my face would have been beetroot red, steam pouring from my ears. Instead, I gnashed my teeth and punched the steering wheel over and over before I got myself back under control. I was doing it again. The thing I'd just said I wouldn't do. Letting my mum take me over, letting her get in my way. I had a job to do, something important, and I was lagging far behind.

I started the Porsche, got the engine roaring, and took off towards the address I'd given Sallow.

Marie hadn't been at the caravan, which meant either Sallow or Kirklander had the correct address. I'd been asleep for hours, the chances of Marie still sitting in one of the other two locations undiscovered were slim at best, but that didn't mean she was dead. Didn't mean the first third of the bounty had been claimed. Marie Lendle was a shifter. Liyta had said she could turn into something with, *"Large claws and oodles of teeth"*. Something like that wasn't about to go easy into the night. Who's to say she wouldn't have come out on top, even?

Sure, if she'd killed Sallow, chances are she would have moved on by now, but perhaps I'd find a clue on his grave that led me to her. Or maybe she'd still be there. Maybe she'd think Sallow was the only one on her tail and now she was safe?

Hey, you never know, maybe I'd get lucky, right?

Well, no, I did not get lucky.

I found the dead body of Marie Lendle curled up on the floor of a bungalow in the village of Larksdale, about thirty minutes east of where I'd almost died in an exploding caravan. She looked like a used teabag, all dried out, scrunched up, drained. I crouched next to her brittle corpse, all moisture, all life, drained out of her, and rolled her on to her back. One of her eyes was missing, the other destroyed.

'Shit.'

It looked as though Sallow had managed to strike the first witness down and take her eyeball, as per the contract, ready to claim the first third of the bounty. Part of me was extremely pissed off to be beaten to the punch, another part of me was kind of glad that at least Kirklander hadn't killed her. He was smug enough as it was without being ahead of the game.

Okay, not to worry, Marie was only one of three. The lion's share of the profit was still out there and waiting to be claimed. I was just going to have to make sure I took care of the other witnesses first. Or perhaps I should put Kirklander's plan into action and try and take out the competition.

As I was about to find out, Kirklander and I weren't the only ones to have had that thought.

At first I didn't feel the hand touching my neck; not until the air was sucked from my lungs and the world around me turned from colour to black and white.

'Say goodbye, normal.'

The voice sounded distant, like it was coming from another room, not from right behind me. I recognised it, though, and realised the danger I was in. Sallow was draining the life out of me.

I half-lurched, half-fell forwards, pulling away from Sallow's killer touch.

'Do not fight Sallow. Accept your fate.'

I twisted around so I was on my back, my limbs all pins and needles, and scrambled away across the floor.

'Coming at me from behind, Sallow? Kinky.'

Sallow ran at me, hands raised, ready to grab hold and do to me what he'd already done to Marie Lendle. Yeah, bollocks to that. I rolled to one side, striking out with a heavy boot and connecting with his knee. Sallow let loose a very satisfying grunt of pain as he staggered to one side, clutching his leg.

'You will pay for that.'

'Not likely, you wet quilt.'

I hopped to my feet, fists raised, tattoos humming with

arcane power. 'You know, Kirklander wanted to team up with me and take you out. I turned him down.'

'Then Kirklander is smarter than you.'

'Okay, I was willing to let trying to kill me slide, but now you're fucking asking for it.'

I ran at him, pulling off my leather jacket as I did so. He swung a fist at me, but I caught it with my jacket and spun around to his back. Once I had him where I wanted him, I grabbed his other arm and knotted the jacket, binding his wrists together. The leather insulated me from his power; so long as he couldn't touch bare skin, he couldn't pull off his party trick.

'How's this for kinky?' I breathed into his ear, right before I ploughed his face into a wall.

Sallow went down like a sack of potatoes, the jacket slipping from my grip as he went. I darted towards him and tried to bring my boot down on his ribs, but Sallow was more gymnastic than I gave him credit for, and rolled back, legs over head. My foot struck the floor with such force that I almost broke my own ankle. Slightly embarrassed, I hobbled towards Sallow as he freed his hands and tossed my jacket aside.

'Enough!' he said, pulling a gun from somewhere in his figure-hugging leather outfit.

'Oh, now that's not fair,' I said. 'You have hands that can drain the life out of a person *and* a gun? Where's the class in that?'

'It matters not how a base normal like you dies, only that you are dead.'

He pointed the gun at me and my every muscle tensed, ready to jump, to run, to get the hell out of there.

'What?' said Sallow, his face a mask of confusion.

I wavered. Was this some sort of trick? He had a gun, why wasn't he filling me full of lead already?

I got my answer pretty swiftly.

Sallow coughed and blood exploded from his mouth, landing on the floor between us with a wet slap.

'Uh, Sallow?'

He looked down at his feet. 'No. No!'

I stepped forward and tried to see what Sallow saw. It took a second or two before I noticed them.

Before I saw the shadows.

There were five of them, stretching out in different directions from his feet. How did he have five shadows, and why did each of them look as though it was being cast by a different shaped person?

The answer, of course, was because none of the five shadows were being cast by Sallow.

'Help me!' he squealed. Those would be the last words he spoke.

I watched in horror, slowly backing away as the unnatural shadows destroyed Sallow's body. He tried to run but couldn't; all he could do was thrash and scream and beg for mercy as his flesh tore open, wide rips unzipping across his face and neck. His outfit turned to whirling rags as his torso was sliced and ripped and gouged. His limbs cracked, bending in impossible directions, snapping in half and folding back on themselves. The destruction of his body was quick and rabid. Within a few horrifying seconds, Sallow was dead.

9

I won't lie, watching what happened to Sallow, the sheer terror on his face, the sounds his body made as his bones broke and his flesh tore, gave me a bad case of the willies.

I didn't hang around. As soon as I regained control of my legs I turned and ran. Ran from dead Marie Lendle and Sallow's mangled corpse, leapt into my car, and stamped on the accelerator with such force it's a wonder it didn't turn to dust.

What the hell happened in there? Those shadow thingies? They reminded me a little of the Wraiths I'd encountered whilst hunting for a missing soul for the Long Man, but worse, if possible.

Were they something to do with the dead witness? Had the prosecutor employed a more high-end boobytrap than the pressure mat bomb that almost cooked my hide? Some kind of avenging spirits maybe? Just about anything's possible in the world I run in. The only real rule is that there are no rules.

It didn't take long for the horror of what I'd seen to

recede enough for annoyance to take its place. About a mile and half, in fact. I pounded the steering wheel, sounding the horn. Damn it. One witness down, one third of the pot gone. Sallow had taken Marie Lendle's eyeball, and without that, I couldn't claim the bounty. Thanks to those shadow monsters, my meal ticket was packed into Sallow's scrunched-up meat and bone ball, and from what I saw, anything he had on him—certainly anything as delicate and squishable as an eyeball—would be little more than a gloopy stain by now. Not the sort of thing that Jenkins & Jenkins would accept as proof of a job well done.

I did briefly consider turning the car around and seeing —hope beyond hope—whether I could rescue the eyeball from Sallow's remains, but a mental replay of what the shadows had done to him drop-kicked that idea out of my mind. I had no intention of facing off against those things, not now, not ever. So long as there was still two-thirds of the pot up for grabs, there was no sense putting myself in that kind of danger.

God damn it.

Okay. Clear head needed. Most of the money was still on the table, so I was still a long way from defeated. Yes, getting a chunk of that money meant taking on a demon, but then again, my competition had just been cut by a third. Now it was just me and Kirklander left in the game, and I was a better player than him. Way better. This was the life I'd chosen, and I'd chosen it because I was good at it. I wouldn't let myself be second best, not ever. I'm the number one killer in this town, ask around and folks will tell you: Erin Banks don't shoot blanks.

The money would be mine. Oh yes, indeed.

Speaking of money, my phone starting vibrating in my

pocket. I pulled it out to see ALIVE JENKINS on the screen. I sighed and hit Answer.

'I'm busy, AJ.'

'AJ...? Oh, Alive Jenkins! I get it. Brother, she calls me Alive Jenkins because I'm the alive one and you're the dead one. Isn't that funny?'

I rolled my eyes as I heard the ghost of his brother throwing some choice insults in Alive Jenkins' direction.

'Kind of busy right now, guys,' I said. 'Less than forty-eight hours on the clock and I still have two witnesses left to brutally murder.'

'Did you say *two* witnesses?'

'Yup. First one is now an ex-witness.'

'Then congratulations are in order. One third of the bounty is yours, as soon as you hand over the eyeball, of course. Rules are rules.'

'Yeah, that's a thing I'll definitely be doing, because I'm the one that killed her,' I replied, vamping a bit. It hurt on a primal level that one third of the bounty seemed to be beyond reach. One third of the money, just sitting there, unclaimable.

Well. We'd have to see about that.

'Anything else?' I asked. 'Lovely as it is to hear from you, AJ.'

'Ha! AJ. I do like that. I'm going to be using that all the time.' More swear words in the background from DJ. 'Good work so far, Miss Banks. Two witnesses left to go and two days left to take them out. You're on track to ruin this trial.'

'Easy work,' I said, trying not to picture Sallow's recent, horrifying death.

'Good, good, but please bear this in mind as you go forward: we cannot allow this case to go to trial with even a single witness in the prosecution's pocket. Do you understand? Jenkins & Jenkins are not in the business of losing cases.'

'Well then, lucky for you that *I'm* not in the business of letting my targets live.'

That seemed like a pretty cool sentence to leave things on, so I ended the call and pushed down on the accelerator.

O n to the next witness.

I needed to check in with Cupid and see how he was getting on with finding Jarvis Fuller, the magician. Back in Brighton, I pulled the Porsche into the garage I rented at the bottom of my street, and got out my phone. Fingers a blur, I fired off a message to Cupid, offering up an extra note or two if he got me something before the day was done. Kirklander would no doubt be after Jarvis already, so I couldn't risk taking my foot off the gas. I needed to know where Jarvis Fuller was holed up, and soon.

I pocketed my phone and reached a hand to the car door to open it, but something gave me pause. I got the sudden feeling that I wasn't alone in the garage. For a moment, I wondered if it was Kirklander, lurking in the shadows, ready to take out the competition. I'd turned down his offer to kill Sallow, maybe he'd decided that made me fair game. This was work, after all. Nothing personal, as he always said. I didn't think he'd actually murder me to keep my hands off any of "his" bounty—not like he would with any other assassin—but I reckon by this point we all know he'd have nothing against taking me out of the picture some other way. Knock me out, imprison me for a time, whatever it took to clear the way for him to collect those last two eyeballs.

'If that's you, Kirklander, I'm gonna rip your dick off.'

Silence.

'Kirk?'

It wasn't him.

I leaned forward, the steering wheel pressing against my chest, squinting through the windshield.

There was a dark shape stretching up the bare brick back wall of my garage, directly in front of the car bonnet.

'Oh, shit,' I muttered, and with good reason.

I glanced around the garage, twisting in my seat, trying to see if there was an intruder that might, somehow, be casting the shadow. But no, I was alone. Just me and the shadow. It knew where I parked, and had been waiting for me to return. Waiting to give me a taste of the same fate Sallow had suffered.

'Okay, okay...'

No need to panic. Well, no need just yet. I just had to slip out of the car, bolt for the open garage door, and leg it away. Hopefully the shadow didn't move as fast as I did when I was juiced up on tattoo power.

I reached for the door handle, my eyes glued to the perfectly still black shape on the wall ahead of me. A click as I pulled the handle and the door popped open slightly. The shadow didn't move. Could it hear the door open? Could it see what I was up to?

Time to boogie. I turned and pushed the door open. I had one foot on the ground before I noticed the second shadow, stretched across the ground just inches from where my foot had landed.

'Fuck.'

I yanked my leg back inside like the floor was lava, and slammed the door shut. Another second and the shadow would have latched on, and that would've been all she wrote.

'Okay, shadow on the wall, shadow on the floor. No big deal. Nothing to worry about. You've got this.'

I shuffled over the gear stick and flopped down on the passenger seat, heart hammering in my chest, obviously not convinced by my little motivational speech.

'Let's try this again, shall we?'

I played it smarter this time and looked before I leaped. I peered through the passenger window and saw yet another shadow lurking on the ground. The bastards had me surrounded.

It was around about this point that I realised I was being a complete idiot. Why was I trying to jump out and run when I was in a bloody car? Cursing my own stupidity, I hopped back over to the driver's seat and reached for the key, ready to spark up the engine and back the hell out of there.

The shadow on the wall in front of me suddenly decided it was done playing possum. It must have known what I was up to, because before I could turn the key, it surged forward, across the bonnet and into the car itself. A shadow cast on no surface, hanging two-dimensional in the air before me. Luckily for me, I was souped up by my tattoos, my reflexes on red alert, my body ready for anything. The moment the shadow darted forward, my body went into autopilot. The driver's side door flew open and I threw myself out, sailing over the shadow that lurked on the ground and landing in a heap on the garage floor.

No time to count my bruises. I hopped up on to my feet and ran for the open garage door. Only it wasn't open anymore.

'Bollocks.'

I yanked at the handle, trying to open the door, but it wouldn't budge.

'Fucking, fuckity, fuck!' I said, correctly.

I turned, back pressed against the door, to see the three shadows—the one that had entered the car and the two on the ground—snaking towards me. They were vipers and I was a cornered mouse. Except I wasn't just any mouse.

No.

I was Mighty Mouse!

(Christ. Please pretend I didn't just say that...)

I turned to the garage door and struck out, my tattoos burning furiously, my knuckles leaving four matching divots in the metal. I struck out in the same place with my left hand, then my right, over and over. How much time did I have? Were the shadows already latched on? The skin on my hands split under the force of the blows I dealt the garage door, my knuckles cracked and popped, but I didn't cry out, I just carried on my furious assault until, finally, with a screech of anguished metal, the door erupted and I dove through the wound I'd created.

I rolled as I landed and came back up, looking at the ground, turning round and around like a dog chasing its own tail, trying to see if I was trailing any shadows that weren't mine.

I was all clear.

'Ha! That shit might work on a newb like Sallow, but I'm Erin fucking Banks.'

The three shadows emerged through the hole in the garage door, slithering across the twisted metal and across the tarmac, winding towards me.

Okay, less lip and more running.

I burst into Black Cat Ink, heart smashing against my ribcage, straining for breath as I stumbled down the steps, pushed through the curtain, and collapsed on the couch. I'd sprinted non-stop from the garage to Parker's tattoo parlour, and judging by my exhaustion, plus the fact that my hands hadn't healed, my tattoos were more or less played out.

'You know, girl, most folk say "Hello"' when they come in here,' said Parker, perched behind the counter, drumming his fingers on its wooden top.

'Hello,' I stammered, holding up a pair of hands that looked like two mangled steaks.

Now the adrenalin was wearing off, my body had decided it was time to let me know about the massive amounts of pain I'd inflicted upon myself. My hands were fucked. Fingers broken and twisted, knuckles mashed, hands so covered in blood it looked as though I'd dipped my fists into a tin of red paint. I clenched my teeth and tried to will some ambient magic into my tattoos, tried to juice them up just enough to numb the pain, but it was no use. I needed another dose of Parker's ink.

He sighed. He might have been unable to see what I'd done to myself, but he sensed enough to know I wasn't there on a social call.

'Get in the chair, woman.'

Using my elbows, I pushed myself back up on my feet, then tried to take off my t-shirt, which was more than a little difficult with two mashed hands.

'A little help?' I said. 'Hands are fucked, you're going to have to undress me.'

Parker grunted and grimaced as he took off my top.

'And the rest,' I said.

He shook his head and undid the clasp on my bra.

'You know,' I managed, as my stomach churned and my legs shook with pain, 'most men are happier about getting my tits out.'

'Just get in the chair.'

I flopped on to it, trembling, skin glistening with sweat.

As magic swirled from Parker's sightless eyes and into the needle that retraced the runes tattooed into my flesh, he got to questioning me.

'You claim any eyeballs yet?'

'No,' I said through gritted teeth.

Not only did my hands hurt like a bastard, now my whole body was under attack. The tattoos would heal me once they were properly grafted, but not before they made me suffer. 'Sallow got the first one, but he's dead now.'

Parker paused. 'And you didn't get the eye from him?'

'It was a little beyond retrieval, Parks.'

He tutted and carried on. 'Lost money, Banks. Sloppy. So what happen to you, eh? Sallow do this?'

'Ha! He wishes. No, this was, well, some shadows came after me.'

'Shadows?'

'Yeah, they killed Sallow, then I found some waiting for me at my garage.'

'Prosecution really don't want you stopping this case if they called up that kinda artillery.'

Didn't I know it? Jesus, they really weren't messing around. They'd do whatever it took to stop us before we put their witnesses in the dirt.

'How do I kill a shadow?' I asked.

'Oh, it's simple.'

'Good.'

'You don't.'

'Not so good.'

'Listen, these things, these shadows, they're not to be messed with. They're called shades. They're kinda like hunting dogs, and once they've got your scent, they'll chase you down relentlessly. They don't stop. Don't get tired. Park your arse for too long and they'll have you. They might not be the fastest, but they'll follow you to the edge of the Earth, and once they latch onto you? Well, it's bye bye Birdie, you get me?'

Awesome.

'There must be some way to stop these shade things? I mean, everything has a weakness, right?'

'Oh, there is a way, only it's well beyond you, girl.'

'Rude.'

'Truth. It'd take a master of the Uncanny to stop 'em. All you can do is try and stay ahead of them until the job is done and they're called off.'

Parker stepped off the pedal and the tattoo gun wound down. I gulped and shuddered as the fresh ink began to glow. Magic soaked into the runes and went to work fixing my hands, fusing the bones, repairing broken skin. I sat up and reached for my bra and top, making myself decent again.

'Thanks, Parks.'

'How's your mum?'

Unbelievable.

'I should never have showed Lana this place...' I replied, swerving the question.

Parker shivered and sat bolt upright.

'What is it?'

'I dunno... I think...' He turned to me, his entirely white eyes fixing on mine. 'Count the shadows.'

I looked at the chequerboard floor. Nothing unusual

there. I scanned the rest of the parlour, the battered couch, the walls covered in framed paintings, the folding privacy screen... and then I spotted them. 'Uh, Parks, has the coat stand over there always had four shadows?'

'You're asking a blind man, fool.'

'Good point. I think I'm going to exit at speed now.'

'Get the job done, it's the only way to shake them.'

'Will do.'

'And don't lose any more eyeballs, I want my cut.'

'Your concern is overwhelming,' I said, slowly moving towards the steps that led to the exit, my eyes fixed on the coat stand. The shades began to weave, to ripple, on the linoleum floor.

'Maybe running is a good idea now, girl,' said Parker.

I bolted for the stairs as the shades swarmed towards me.

'Shit, shit, shit!'

'Faster, Banks!' said Parker, his voice giving me an extra shove as I bounded up the steps and threw open the door to the street. I could hear the shades hissing as they slithered up the stairs after me. I looked back to see them just a few seconds behind. Unfortunately, I turned back to face the way I was heading too late, and collided with a man passing by the parlour. The two of us crashed to the ground in an ungainly heap.

'Watch where you're going, you idiot!' the man yelled.

I ignored the insult as I scrambled away from him. 'Get out the way!'

He looked at me, confused for a second, then his eyes widened and he coughed a glob of blood on the pavement. The shades had passed over him—the person blocking their way—and had taken a few bites as they went. The man screamed and thrashed, but that only seemed to excite the shades. They hit pause on their pursuit of me, bloodlust drawing their attention elsewhere, blinding them to the job at hand. The screaming man was chum in the water, making the sharks lose their minds.

I should have run. This was a perfect opportunity to put some space between me and them. I stood, ready to go, but something made me stop. What was that gnawing at me? A conscience?

Shit.

Dangerous thing to have in this game.

'Oi, shades, it's me you want, right?'

The shadows reared up to look at me, two-dimensional, black shapes weaving like cobras. I took a step toward them. 'Come on then, dinner's ready.'

The man I'd collided with shuffled away, bleeding from a few places, but otherwise fine. Alive.

'Get out of here,' I hissed. 'Go on!'

The man nodded, in pain and completely bewildered, traumatised by something he'd never be able to get to grips with. He turned and hobbled away as fast as his badly lacerated legs would let him.

I'd stopped the shades killing an innocent man, which should have made me feel good, I supposed. But there was no time for that. I turned, and with my tattoos feeding speed into my legs, ran like my arse was on fire.

10

The shades made my job a whole lot trickier. Not only did I have a short amount of time to find and kill two witnesses, not only did I have to pip Kirklander to the punch, now I had to keep on the move or else a bunch of killer shadows would scrunch me up like a used tissue. At least, after my experience with the man I'd bumped into outside of Parker's, I knew the shades could be distracted. That they could be pushed off course, that was something, right?

As I ran, I realised I was actually smiling. Smiling at all the danger piling up on me. Yeah, I might have a few issues. But life is a lot more interesting when it can be snatched away at any moment, isn't it? That's what I think, anyway. Put me in peril and I'm happy as a dog with two dicks.

I'd lost sight of the shades chasing me, but they'd still be on my tail and I couldn't keep running around like a hopped-up goose, I needed transport. There was no way I was going to risk going back to my garage to see if I could rescue the Porsche. No doubt a shade or two would be waiting close-by, just in case. No, fresh wheels were required. A quick glance up and down a quiet side road, then I punched through the passenger-side window of a small, blue car and let myself in. The insides smelled like sweat and cigarettes mixed with old takeaway meals. Lovely stuff.

Okay then, transport acquired. Now I could keep on the move without wearing my legs down to nubs. I felt safer inside the car too, now I had time to think, to plan, to get the job done. I rolled around the streets of Brighton, firing off message after message to Cupid (kids, don't text and drive, okay?) until he finally responded and we arranged a meeting spot.

'About time,' I said, pulling up and opening the passenger side door. Cupid clambered into the passenger seat.

'Aw, what happened to the Porsche?' he asked, pulling a cigar from his nappy and lighting it.

'A bunch of shadows are sitting on it.'

'You what?'

'Forget it. What have you got for me?'

Cupid grinned, showing off two rows of tiny yellow teeth. 'Oh, I got all the news, honey.'

I shivered. 'Call me honey again and I'll punch you right in your cute, round belly.'

'Jeez, you on the rag, or what?'

Christ, what a little shit. 'Just get on with it,' I said, pulling away from my parking spot and rejoining traffic.

'No big deal, I only got the location of Marie Lendle. You're welcome, as is your money.' Cupid reached a grasping hand towards me.

'Yeah, I already got that address, and Marie is deader than your chances of getting any cash out of me for that useless titbit.'

'Aw, come on! Could've let me know, maybe? I've been flying all over the place doing your donkey work for nothing.'

'All right, Mister Sensitive. Here,' I handed him a ten pound note, he took it with a look of disgust.

'I wouldn't wipe my arse with this.' He grumbled something under his breath and stuffed the note into his nappy anyway.

'Anything else,' I asked, 'or are you wasting my time?'

Cupid crossed his arms and jutted out his bottom lip. It was as annoying as it was adorable.

'Look, I'm sorry, okay? Next time I'll keep you in the loop a bit more.'

Cupid shrugged like he wasn't bothered. I sighed and handed over a second ten pound note. His eyes lit up and he snatched it from me.

'All better?' I asked.

'For now, toots.'

'Is that all you've got for me?'

Cupid wavered his hand, 'Kinda. Maybe. Maybe not.'

'Get on with it or I'm tossing you through that broken window.'

'I might have a lead on a second witness.'

'Jarvis Fuller?'

'That's the pony.'

Okay, witness number two, a low-level wizard according to Liyta.

'Spill the beans, baby-man.'

'Thing is, the information sounds dodgy to me, but it's from a very reliable source. Well, source who heard it from their source who overheard someone else whispering about it. Only thing is, what they told me sounded a bit... well, impossible.'

'Bit rich coming from a flying baby.'

Cupid frowned. He took a drag of his cigar before blowing out a cloud of grey smoke and turning to me. 'So you ever hear of Other London?'

I t's fair to say that Cupid's question caught me off guard.

Other London.

I'd only heard of it recently, after the soul collection gig for the Long Man. I'd been told about it by a man named Carlisle. A man that I'd met the night my brother James was kidnapped. I'd thought he might be involved, but it turned out I'd only run into him by chance. Crossed paths while I was lost and wandering strange streets I didn't recognise. Strange streets that Carlisle claimed were part of Other London, a hidden place that had since been cut off from the ordinary world. Other London was lost, that's what Carlisle had said. He told me that tragedy had befallen it, and that any entrances to the secret city were now gone.

According to Cupid, his source had informed him that Jarvis Fuller was hiding somewhere in Other London. That the magician had been fascinated with the place and had located a last remaining door a year or so back, only telling one or two people he could trust. Clearly one of these trusted people had, at some point, broken that trust. Now that Jarvis was in need of a hiding place, he'd obviously thought it the best place to hunker down until the trial, confident that no one else would find the lone entrance that led to him. Confident that no one would even think of the place as it was well known to be out of reach. It seemed he needed to find better people to whisper his secrets to. And so we drove to London. To get to Other London.

I drove with my jaw so tightly clenched I gave myself a headache. I'd found myself in Other London when I was a kid, back when James was taken, but I'd been told there was no going back. If what Cupid told me was true and there was a way in, I'd be able to walk the streets of the last place I'd seen my brother. Perhaps he was still there. Despite the years, despite the tragedy Carlisle claimed had befallen the place, maybe... maybe I'd be able to shine a light on my brother's disappearance. Maybe I'd find James.

I knew it was stupid. Chances were he was long gone, and if he wasn't, the idea that he'd still be there seemed fanciful at best. But hey, hope is a powerful drug.

'It's over there,' said Cupid, pointing a stubby finger at a boarded-up betting shop on the outskirts of Ealing, London.

'You're sure?'

'That's what I was told.'

I pulled over and stepped out, Cupid hovering by my side, his little wings flapping like a hummingbird's.

'So the entrance to a magical, lost city is through a manky, old betting shop?'

Cupid shrugged and tossed away his used-up cigar.

'So what now?' I asked.

'You go in, I guess.'

I stepped towards the shop, only for Cupid to stay where he was. 'You coming?'

'Not likely. You don't pay me enough to flutter my way into mystical sunken cities.'

'Then why travel all this way with me?'

'Good casino a few streets away. Thanks for the lift.'

'What? I'm not a bloody cab service.'

'Good luck in there, text me if you don't get dead.'

Cupid turned and flew up into the sky at a speed that belied his rotund little figure.

'Okay then. Other London.'

I shoved the locked door and it burst open. I looked over both shoulders, then stepped into the building. It stank of mould inside, of decay, of rotting things. As my eyes adjusted to the gloom I saw old chairs, broken tables, a smashed-up counter, but no secret streets.

I pulled out the piece of paper Cupid had handed to me. On it was scrawled a mantra I was supposed to repeat.

'How many times?'

'I dunno, until it works, I guess.'

'That's what I like about working with you, Cupid, your attention to detail.'

I read the words out loud. 'Believe there is a door, and a door there shall be.'

Over and over I said the words, my only audience the rats and the spiders.

'Believe there is a door, and a door there shall be. Believe there is a door, and a door there shall be. Believe there is a door, and a door there shall be.'

I could feel my skin tingling, like static electricity was washing over me.

'Believe there is a door, and a door there shall be.'

And then there was. A small, green, wooden door on a wall that, a heartbeat before, had been plain plaster.

'Well, fuck a duck.'

I approached the door and crouched before it. The door was tiny, only reaching as high as my hips. It looked old. Much older than the betting shop that housed it. A brass knocker, coated in rust, sat in the middle, and above it, rather than a house number, were two brass letters, nailed into place. An 'O' and an 'L'.

'Other London,' I whispered.

I thought about my mum, laid up in bed, broken, unconscious.

I thought about my baby brother, floating away in a ball of magic.

I thought about a face with piercing red eyes.

And then I reached out a hand and pushed open the door.

'Here goes something,' I said, and squeezed through the opening.

I crawled out onto a cobbled road.

I stood and turned to look back at the opening I'd come through. On this side, the door wasn't supported by a wall, it simply hung in the air, stood in nothing. The small door closed behind me, blocking the view of the rotting innards of the old shop.

I took a look around. Took in the cramped street, the old buildings pressing in at me, bowed and uneven, like rows of crooked teeth. It was as though I'd stepped from modern London back into Victorian times. I half expected to see the cast of *Oliver* marching down the street, dancing a wee jig and singing a merry song about child poverty.

Was this real? Was I actually in Other London?

I inhaled deeply. The air was stale and heavy with dust. It felt still, like a world holding its breath.

I walked forward slowly, carefully, taking it all in. I'd been here. I'd been to this place, I knew it. Even though I didn't recognise the street, or the buildings that leaned forward as though about to collapse on top of me, I was greeted with a stomach-churning sense of déjà vu. On one of these streets, Carlisle had stepped out of the shadows to greet me as I wandered, lost, alone, in tears.

I wondered what had happened to this place, why it had been sealed off for so long. I couldn't see any evidence of people living there. Just like the betting shop I'd walked through to get there, Other London was no longer in use. So what drove everyone away? Why was it abandoned? And why were the entrances lost for so long?

I'd have gone on wandering and wondering for hours, but I was about to be interrupted. Just as I had with the boobytrapped caravan, I'd allowed myself to become distracted, and lost sight of the danger I was in. I failed to notice when I was joined by a second figure, but he soon caught my attention when his magic lifted me off my feet and deposited me headfirst into the side of a house.

'Prepare to die,' roared Jarvis Fuller, his hands boiling with angry, red magic.

11

L ike a cowardly goalkeeper I dived off to one side, away from the churning hoop of flame that turned a patch of nearby brickwork into rubble and dust.

I was angry. Not just at the fact I'd been smashed into a wall and shot at, but because I hadn't been given a chance to tell Jarvis Fuller just how corny his, "Prepare to die!" line was, and now the timing was all wrong. I mean, come on. *Prepare to die*? I've heard better dialogue in *Keeping Up With the Kardashians*.

Not that I've ever seen that show. Of course.

Shut up.

I jumped and rolled again as another fistful of crackling, strobing magic was unleashed in my direction.

'There's no need for this, Jarvis,' I said, 'let's stop and have a chat. I'm only here to murder you.'

My cunning ploy did not work. The cobbles caught me as another blast of magic clipped my heel and sent me spinning. The street whirled drunkenly over me, the sky switching places with the ground. I scrambled up to my feet and jumped behind the front wall of a house to catch my breath. I clenched my fists as magic soaked into my tattoos, filling me with strength, making me feel sharp, strong, *alive*. Jarvis might be able to throw concussive blasts of magic, but he was still a low-level wizard, no more powerful than Kirklander, and I'd dealt with him on more than one occasion.

'You'd do this for Liyta?' asked Jarvis. 'You'd ignore her crimes just for a payday? All the innocent people she's toyed with, she's pushed to take their own lives. Children, even!'

Hey, I'd judge me too, but money soothes a guilty conscience better than booze.

'I can get you money,' he said, a quaver to his voice.

'Bit of a step down from, "Prepare to die", isn't it? Where are your balls, man?'

'It doesn't need to go down this way,' he said, ignoring me. 'I can pay you more than whatever the defence is paying.'

'Tempting J-Man, but I'm a professional. The moment I turn on an employer is the moment I never get hired again.'

The wall I was behind shook as Jarvis tossed more magic in the direction of my voice.

'There's my boy,' I cheered.

I clenched my teeth, pulling more and more magic into me. I was done hiding and through playing around. I had to get close to him, and there was only one way I was going to do that. I had to be tough enough to take a little punishment as I closed the distance to my prey.

I grabbed a chunk of brick that had been blasted loose, and tossed it in one direction before bolting from the other side of the wall. As predicted, Jarvis went twisting in the direction of the brick, and tossed a blast of magic at the sound it made as it struck the ground.

I ran for him.

Head down, fists ready, tattoos *burning*.

Jarvis realised his mistake and turned to me as I charged him. He stepped back, startled, and flapped a hand in my direction. Caught by surprise, his aim was poor, and the blast sailed over my head.

I was seconds away from him now.

Another blast. This one hit me in the chest, but I was so strong, so full of momentum, that it barely knocked me back a step, barely caused me to catch my breath, and then it was too late. My shoulder struck Jarvis' chest and I heard his rib cage crack. Down we went to the ground, me on top, Jarvis letting loose a startled yelp of pain as he struck the cobbles.

He lashed out at me with his fists, animal fear overcoming him, too panicked to string together the necessary phrases for a spell. It wouldn't have mattered if he could. I was too strong for him—way too strong—he could struggle all he liked, but it was no use. He was a kitten trying to swat away a rhino. I grinned as he wriggled beneath me. I was powerful. I was the hunter. I was the killer. I yelled out in triumph as my fist met his nose, then his jaw, his neck, his mouth.

Jarvis stopped fighting back.

His face was pulp, his breath a ragged, wet slurp. He was clinging to life, but I was ready to stomp on his fingertips that clung to the cliffedge and send him hurtling to the hungry sea.

'Don't... not for... not for her...' slurred Jarvis, his words bubbling up between split, bloodied lips.

I gripped his skull between my hands and twisted, snapping his neck. Ending his life.

I may have mentioned this before, but I'm no hero, okay? I'm a killer. A murderer for hire. As far as I was concerned, the bloodied corpse I was straddling was nothing more than evidence of a job well done.

Speaking of evidence...

I pulled a leather pouch from my jacket pocket, and with my free hand, dug my fingers into one of Jarvis Fuller's eye sockets and yanked the eyeball from its socket. The jellied orb emerged with a wet *schtuck* noise before catching on its optic nerve like a paddleball on a length of elastic.

What do you mean, gross? What do you want, a fainting couch?

I severed the optic nerve with my knife and tucked the extracted eyeball into my pouch. One third of the bounty was now mine. I smiled and stood, pocketing the pouch.

'Bad luck, Kirklander. Two down and no cash for you.'

I stabbed out the corpse's other eyeball so Kirklander couldn't claim it. Probably a bit over cautious given that he had no idea how to get to Other London, but you can't be too careful in this game.

I stood and stepped away from Jarvis' broken body. I was eager to explore Other London, but I knew there was more money out there yet, and not much time left to claim it. Now I knew the way in, now I knew that it even existed, I could come back another time, once my work was done. I turned to head in the direction of the exit when something made me freeze.

'No...'

My heart hopped into my throat. I had three shadows.

'Shit. No. No, no, no...' I backed away, tried to back away, but the three shadows followed me. Not just followed me, mirrored me, like it was me who was casting them, though I knew it wasn't.

Stupid. That's what I was. Stupid and reckless and it's a wonder I'd lasted this long without ending up six feet under. Of course there would be shades close at hand. Someone in the prosecution knew where Jarvis was holed up, so when they sent the shades after the assassins hired to take out the three witnesses, of course some would be lurking close to Jarvis.

I should have been aware of that likelihood and kept a lookout, but I didn't, and now I was royally screwed. I crouched and tried to bat them off, to dislodge the shades that clung to me, but it was as useless as trying to beat away my own shadow. So I ran. Taking turn after turn blindly. Tattoos glowing, I sprinted down the streets of Other London, panic overwhelming me, but it was no use. They were latched on to me now, I couldn't run away, it was like they were part of me.

I screamed as I felt the skin on my back begin to tear.

This was it.

Parker had told me there was no way I could beat the shades, not once they'd attached to me. Strength and speed were of no use, I needed magic. Strong, skilled magic. Magic beyond what I could pull from the air.

I turned a corner, only to find myself back where I'd started and almost tripping over the dead body of Jarvis Fuller. Soon enough there would be two corpses in Other London, his and mine. I stopped running and yelled, my voice echoing up the empty streets, off the cobbles, off the Victorian buildings that leaned in like they were angling for a closer look at the fresh wounds opening up on me. At the blood pouring from my lacerated body.

I fell and felt my kneecaps crack against stone. If this was how I was going to go out, I wouldn't give my killers the satisfaction of tears. If I could have prevented myself from screaming as my body was taken apart I would have done so, but that much was impossible. Screaming was okay, though. Screaming was for warriors.

It was fitting really, dying there, in Other London, where

it all started. Where my journey into the Uncanny Kingdom first began. The me I became, the me I was now, was born running along these streets, searching for my kidnapped brother. And now it would end there, in that same place. Full circle. Sort of neat, I supposed.

I closed my eyes and waited for death to numb the pain.

'*Klatu, Halak, Faloon, Halbre!*' said a voice like a meteor tearing through silk.

A sudden wind struck me and blew me on to my back.

'What the shit?' I cried, opening my eyes to see a tall, thin figure in an almost floor-length purple coat looming over me. 'Carlisle?'

'You can stop bleeding, now,' he said, eyeing me with his cool, dark eyes.

'Bollocks!' I yelled, scrabbling around, remembering the shadows that were busy murdering me. Only there were no shadows, and I seemed to be very much un-murdered. I pushed myself up and leaned back against the wall of a building, a little unsteady. 'Where'd they go?'

'Where I sent them,' Carlisle replied. 'You know, most would offer the person who saved their life their heartfelt thanks. Even a life as meaningless as yours.'

'You got rid of the shades? How?'

'With ease, and dare I say it, no small amount of style.' Carlisle gave his coat a little flourish and for a moment I caught sight of the lining; it was as though he had a sparkling galaxy sewn into it.

'Your work, I presume?' asked Carlisle, standing over the one-eyed corpse and prodding it with the toe of his boot.

'A witness,' I said, clenching my teeth as my tattoos got to work sealing up the wounds the shades had inflicted upon me. Carlisle's eyes flicked from the corpse to me as I healed.

'Impressive,' he said. 'Crude, obviously, and painful, no

doubt. It's a wonder you can take the burden, surely it must cause your body agony to have those runes reapplied over and over. Why, your very bones must *ache*.'

'Aw, I didn't know you cared.'

'An observation, not sympathy.'

I wiped the sweat from my brow and reached into my jacket, pulling out a small plastic canister of pills. I poured three into my mouth and swallowed them down dry. 'How did you know I was here?'

'Young lady, I have eyes all over.'

'So an eaves told you?'

'Perhaps,' he replied, with a small smile teasing his thin lips. 'After our last meeting I made sure I would know of your comings and goings.'

'Paranoid, much?'

'Paranoia is for the feeble. I like to think of myself as *thorough*.'

I paced back and forth, agitated, but Carlisle did not move. He stood quite still, unconcerned, confident, his eyes never leaving mine. I knew he could tear me limb from limb if he wanted to, but being massively outgunned has never stopped me before.

'You said this place didn't exist anymore. That it was lost.'

'I believe I also told you that I was a liar.'

'So you knew?'

Carlisle sighed. 'Actually, no. As far as I was aware, all the entrances to Other London had been lost. Destroyed. The entrance in Newcastle, in Brighton, in Blackpool, in Edinburgh, and in London itself. All of them and more, gone.'

'Seems like you're not the only liar in town, eh?'

Carlisle's eyes narrowed for a moment, and I couldn't help but smile at his annoyance.

'It would seem so, yes.' He turned his back on me and began to wander in a small circle, taking in all the sights around him. 'It has been a long time since I walked these ancient streets, Erin Banks. Once they were full of people, of noise, of smells. And now...' he paused and rested a foot upon the corpse of Jarvis Fuller, 'now it has all the life of a crypt.'

I wished I could remember more of what I'd seen there. What I'd experienced. My brother was taken to this place, that much I knew for sure. What I still didn't have a bead on was the "why?" and the "who?".

'Why did you save my life?' I asked Carlisle.

He turned to me wearing an expression that left me thinking he'd forgotten for a moment that I was even there. 'Because we are connected now.'

'Because you met me here as a kid?'

'Partly. Your recent visit made me think about that day for the first time in years. It led to me revisiting my memories of what happened here before I found you. Of what happened after. And do you know what I found, assassin?'

'What?' I asked, my heart thumping loud in my ears.

Carlisle opened his arms wide. 'Nothing.'

'Nothing?'

'Absolutely nothing. Like you, my recollections have been taken from me. Stolen. And no one steals from Carlisle.'

Well, now, there was a thing.

'So who stole them?'

'Well, that is the million dollar question, is it not?'

'How was it done?' I asked. 'How does someone go about stealing a memory?'

'How are most things done in our world?'

'Magic.'

'Indeed. Some powerful incantation was used to obscure the truth of that day. An incantation of such sophistication that I had not even realised something was missing until you came to me, all angry-faced and clenched-fisted.'

So whoever was behind James' disappearance had muddled our memories with magic to hide the truth. But why? Why not just kill us?

'So what now?'

Carlisle frowned as he retrieved a bright red apple from his coat pocket and took a crisp bite. He slowly chewed and swallowed before replacing the apple in the pocket.

'Now I take a more active interest in your predicament, assassin. I am Carlisle, once and future king of Uncanny Britain.'

'Come again? Did you say *king*?'

'Anyone who toys with my memories will discover they have made a most fatal mistake,' he declared, steamrollering my question. 'You will be hearing from me, Erin Banks. Oh, yes.'

He swept his coat in a wide arc as he turned upon his heel and strutted away.

'When? Oi, answer me!'

'I have work to do. Until then...' he raised a leather-gloved hand and waved before turning at the end of the street and disappearing from view.

12

It was nighttime by the time I got back to Brighton. I don't remember the drive, I was on autopilot the whole way there, replaying what I'd been through in Other London. The sight of the place. The way it felt. The things Carlisle had told me.

Magic had been used.

On me, on him. Magic to rob us of our memories. To erase the things we'd seen. To protect the identities of whoever had done the meddling.

To do that to me was one thing, I was just a little girl when it happened, a nobody. But to do it to Carlisle? That felt important. That was a big risk, a bold swing. Messing with him meant something. Why did they need this thing hidden so badly that they'd risk corrupting the memory of someone as powerful and ruthless as Carlisle? And who else might they have done the same to? How far did this thing go, whatever the hell this "thing" even was?

And what did any of this have to do with my baby brother?

I only realised where I was when the automatic doors of

the hospital sighed open and I was bathed in the harsh striplights of the reception area. My first thought was to stop, to get out of there. To get back in the stolen car I'd parked outside and head home for some rest.

But my feet wouldn't listen.

So I found myself in the intensive care unit, stood outside the door to a private room, sweat prickling my forehead.

I took a breath, opened the door, and stepped inside. The room had that hand sanitiser alcohol smell that reminded me of those chocolate liqueurs you get at Christmastime. My mother was laid out in the room's only bed, sound asleep next to a vase of flowers and a box of Maltesers, her favourite, still untouched.. The room didn't have a window to let any outside light in, so it was dark inside. The only light came from a dim lamp and the various life support machines that surrounded her, bleeping and purring, monitoring her heart. The same heart I would have listened to once, before she brought me into this world. A world I was barely a part of anymore, thanks to her.

I felt for a chair and sat down beside the bed, watching the dark shape of my sleeping mum as her chest rose and fell. This was the first time I'd shared a room with her in... I couldn't even remember how long. Years. Years and years. Part of me wanted to grab a pillow and hold it over her face until her body went still. Another part wanted to curl up on the bed and fall asleep beside her.

'I went back there, Mum. Back to the place you told me didn't exist. The old-looking place. The secret streets. The place they took James.'

The dark hump in the bed muttered and shifted before falling silent and still.

For a moment I thought she'd woken up, and it felt like

someone had reached into my chest and grabbed me by the heart. I waited for my pulse to return to normal before I spoke again.

'I'm getting closer. I know I am. And I've got a friend now, to help. Well, not a friend. Not really. Someone who'd probably kill me if the mood took him. But still, better than nothing. Better than you.'

I thought back to arriving home that day. The day after James went missing. I didn't remember how I got back there, or where I'd spent the night. All I remembered were red eyes, James floating in a scarlet ball, old streets, and then it was morning and I was stepping back into my home.

After that, came a barrage of reality. I remembered Mum standing there, a hand to her mouth, shoulders racking with hot sobs. I remembered Dad dropping his favourite mug and it cracking in half on the kitchen tiles, spilling tea everywhere. I remembered a police officer crouching down to talk to me, this small, dishevelled girl, a missing person they assumed they'd find alongside my missing brother, if at all.

'Where's James?'

That's what Mum had asked. She'd bolted forward, grabbed me, hugged me, then demanded to know where he was. Not if I was okay, or what had happened, just *Where's James?*

At first I couldn't say anything.

I opened my eyes and I was in a different place, in my room, in my bed. Dad told me I'd passed out. Mum had asked again.

Where's James?
Where's James?
Where's James?

I don't remember her asking after my wellbeing. Any soft words or concern, just questions and anger and frustration. I remember my mum's hand, tight, around my arm as she shook me, her eyes wide, insisting I just tell the truth.

'You're hurting me, Mum,' I'd told her, trying to pull away.

'We just want to know what happened,' said Dad.

In some ways it had felt like they didn't care that I'd come back. That I was safe, unhurt, alive. It felt more like they were disappointed that I was the one who'd showed up. If one of us had to go missing, why James? Why not me?

Yeah, yeah, I know. The selfish, hurt feelings of a child, I've heard that before, what do you want from me? It's not as though things softened with time. All I got were questions and accusations and cold eyes. Once, a month after he'd gone missing, Mum turned to me and asked, 'What did you do with James?'

And there it was.

The awful thing she'd been keeping inside since I'd showed up that morning.

'What did you do with James?'

I ran out of the room and hid in my room, pulling my bed over so it blocked the door. Fighting to stop the tears escaping from my blurred eyes.

She never asked that question again. Didn't need to. It was out there and it was asked over and over in my mind every time she looked at me. Because what was more believable? The nonsense I'd told her about a walking pig? About a creature with burning eyes? About James floating away in a big red bubble? Or was it more believable that an older sibling, jealous of the attention her baby brother was getting, would do something awful? Would get rid of their little sibling and disassociate from the memories. Shove that terrible crime to the furthest recesses of my mind, because reliving it would be too terrible to bear.

For a moment, even I wondered if that's what had happened.

Had I hurt James?

'I believe you,' said Lana as we crouched under a table, the tablecloth hiding us from view.

No, it wasn't pretend. I knew it. Was sure of it. What had happened, what my mind told me had happened—the bits I could remember anyway—was the truth. I knew it. I knew it with a burning certainty, because all I wanted was to find him. To save him. To get revenge.

'How could you think I'd do that, Mum?' I said in the dark of the hospital room. 'To my own brother.' A tear escaped down my cheek and I bit my lip in anger, wiping it away. 'I'm going to find him. I'm going to find James and I'm going to punish anyone who was involved. Not for you, not for Dad, but for James.'

I stood, fists clenched, and stepped away from the bed, worried about what I might do if I got any closer to her. To the woman who brought me into the world but had dared ask me that question.

No, none of this was for her. None of it.

'What am I even doing here?'

I turned and opened the door, allowing a sliver of light from the corridor to snake inside and slither across the bed sheets.

'Erin...?'

I froze.

'Erin is that you?'

I didn't answer, didn't look back. I stepped through the door, closed it, and left the hospital behind.

13

From one place I didn't want to be to another. Yeah, this next meeting was going to make me swallow a whole lot of pride.

'Well, well, well,' said Kirklander as he joined me on a bench by the seafront, 'you were the last person I was expecting a booty call from.'

'Just shut it, will you?'

'Well, well, and thrice well. I knew you'd come to your senses eventually, babe. So, shall we go to my place, or do you want to do this al fresco?'

Christ, it was like he *wanted* me to punch him in the balls.

I scanned the seafront left and right. It was late and drizzling. No one around but the two of us.

'How do you know I haven't lured you here to kill you, like you suggested we do to Sallow?'

Kirklander leaned on his staff and laughed. 'Ha, good one.'

I stood, arms crossed, and gave him the ol' death stare.

'Wait...' he faltered, his backside leaving the bench. 'Is that really why you called me?'

'Relax, dickhead. I asked you here because...'

'Because your lady parts crave my well-above-average man bits?' He sat back down, legs wide, manspreading for Britain.

Oh, he is the *worst*.

'I asked you here because I think we should team up,' I went on, ignoring him. 'For a bit at least.'

Up until that point I'd thought it impossible for Kirklander to look more smug then he already did. I'd been wrong.

'Stop that,' I said, pushing a hand into his face.

'So you want my help taking down Sallow after all, eh?'

'No thanks, that's already done and dusted.'

Kirklander frowned and twirled his staff. 'You killed him already?'

'He's dead, what do you think?' No need to tell him it was the shades that killed Sallow and not me.

'Cold-blooded, baby.'

'Practical.'

Kirk scratched his chin. 'So all the pie is on the table, one half for each of us?'

'Yep. Sallow took the eye of the first witness, but I took it off him when he died,' I replied, bluffing. No need for Kirklander to know the truth, that one third of the bounty was lost already, the eyeball turned to paste. I needed him to believe that I had it so he'd help me. 'I took out the wizard's eye myself. That's two thirds of the bounty in my pocket already.'

Kirklander bowed a little. 'Congratulations. You've bested me so far.'

'So far? You're always a step behind, you cock.'

'Of course I'm a step behind, Erin, that way I get a view of your solid gold arse.'

He waggled his eyebrows at me, and I actually flushed a little, not out of embarrassment, but because I was flattered.

God, he is the worst.

No, *I'm* the worst.

Maybe we belonged together. The two worst people, hand in hand, forever and ever, amen.

Oh, shit, nope. Punt that thought way over the horizon, Banks.

A seagull landed in front of us, hunting for discarded food. Kirklander raised his staff and fired a concussive blast of multi-coloured magic in its direction, smashing it from its perch and sending it into the sea in a squawking cloud of feathers.

'Was that really necessary?'

'Birds are good target practice. Shall we get down to business, then?'

'You haven't heard what I want you for, yet.'

'Besides rocking your world in bed?'

Uuurrrgghhh.

He went on, undeterred by the sour expression I was wearing. 'I imagine, with two of the witnesses dead, that the only target still standing is the one all three of us will have left until last.'

I nodded. 'Gjindor.'

'A demon. Not the kind of thing you take on single-handed if you've got any brains in your skull.'

'A *minor* demon,' I corrected.

'Oh, he'll be a pushover then,' replied Kirklander, sarcastically. 'Piece of piss.'

'We can take out a demon if we work together. You know we can.'

'I don't know anything.'

'At last he admits it.'

Kirklander laughed. 'And what do I get if I agree to team up and we somehow manage to pull off this kamikaze mission?'

'We'll split the entire bounty, fifty-fifty.' Like I said earlier, no need for Kirklander to know that one third of the bounty was lost, and that I'd be double-crossing him later to keep all the cash for myself. That's the sort of information that puts a person off.

'You know,' said Kirklander, taking aim at another seagull foolish enough to land within his range, 'I had been considering swerving the demon, calling this whole job a wash and walking away.'

The seagull screeched as it was cooked by a ball of fire and reduced to a pile of bird bones.

'And now?'

Kirklander spread his arms wide, his green eyes twinkling. 'How can I say no to you, babe?'

I was just about to give him a mouthful about how he'd better stop calling me "babe" if he wanted his dick to remain unknotted, when the second person I'd texted showed up.

'Aw, no, you're not working with this Muppet again?' said Cupid, jabbing a thumb at Kirklander as his little wings slowly lowered him down onto his tiny feet.

'Afraid so,' I replied.

'Great to see you too, *Stu*-pid,' said Kirklander. 'Still not figured out trousers, then?'

Cupid waddled forward, fuming, ready to go at Kirklander, but I stepped between the two, playing peacemaker for once.

'Okay, boys, none of us like each other here, but we've all got a job to do.'

'You don't like me?' said Cupid, genuinely hurt.

'I meant him,' I clarified, bending down to the cherub's level and hooking a thumb at Kirklander. 'I don't like *him*.'

Cupid grumbled and pulled a fresh cigar from his nappy, chomping it between his teeth before striking a match and fouling the sea air.

It's fair to say that Cupid and Kirklander didn't exactly get on. Kirklander had used Cupes' services in the past but then—Kirk being Kirk—had failed to pay up, and no amount of smiles or nice words were going to unfuck that mess. Apparently, those only worked on me.

In my defence, you've no idea how sexy Kirklander is, or how good he is at... well... things.

Moving on...

'Did you find out where the demon is?' I asked Cupid.

He blew a cloud of thick blue smoke in Kirklander's direction, and nodded. 'Have I ever let you down, Banks?'

'Many times. So where are we going?'

Cupid smiled. 'To a bad, bad place...'

14

The Hidden Forest is in an area known as the Peak District, which sits a little over halfway up England, crouched between Manchester and Sheffield. It's a national park; rolling green hills, great big lakes, and all the natural beauty you can stomach.

You won't find the Hidden Forest on any ordnance survey map though. Only those in touch with the Uncanny know it even exists, let alone how to find it. The good news was that I was one of those people, so I knew where to go and how to locate the final witness. The bad news, of course, was that the witness was a demon who would most likely turn me to ash. But there was even worse news: The Peak District was a good five hour drive from Brighton, and since I'd stolen Kirklander's precious Porsche, he and I had to make the entire journey there stuffed into the Mini Cooper he was driving.

'Remind me why we're not taking Sylvia?' he asked.

Sylvia was what he called his Porsche. He named it after the dinner lady he claimed to have lost his virginity to. Can you imagine how good-looking a person has to be to tell you that and remain attractive? We're talking supernaturally attractive.

'I told you already, the car's not safe.'

'I see. And remind me again why it's *your* Porsche now and not *my* Porsche.'

'Because you're a massive prick.'

'Right, right, I remember.' He smiled and I had to bite my tongue to stop myself from laughing.

Five hours, tootling up the motorway, practically thigh to thigh. The sexual tension was so thick you could have planted a flag in it.

A new song came on the radio.

Kirklander pounded the steering wheel excitedly. 'No way! Do you remember this one?' He smiled and turned it up.

Rhiannon by Fleetwood Mac played, making static dance over my skin. 'No,' I replied, bluntly.

'Of course you do, it's the Mac!'

'Yeah, I remember the song, just not for the reason you want me to remember it.'

'Then how do you know you don't remember it for the reason I want you to remember it if you don't remember it?'

'Okay, we're walking down a confusing path here,' I said, making sure to keep my eyes on the view outside and away from his probing eyes. Of course I remembered it. Of course I knew what Kirklander was getting at.

Our first kiss.

So many years ago now. A dingy basement room in a dodgy pub. Wall-to-wall with drunk, sweaty people dancing to music from the '70s. The room was so small, so packed with writhing meat, that the low ceiling dripped with moisture. We'd locked eyes and found ourselves together, his arms around my waist, mine around his neck, staring hungrily into each other's eyes as Stevie Nicks sang about a Welsh Witch.

As our hands began to roam where they shouldn't, he'd leaned down and pressed his lips to mine, our tongues meeting, our bodies pressing together. It gave me a lady-boner just thinking about it.

I leaned across and turned the radio to another station.

'Don't remember a thing, hey?' said Kirklander.

'Shut up,' I shot back.

I checked my phone. Just another four hours to go.

God help me.

T he Mini jerked to a stop and woke me from the slumber I'd slipped into to avoid any more dangerous reminiscing. The last thing I was inter-ested in at that point was picking things up with Kirklander again. Or, if I could help it, ever. If only sticking to that "ever" part wasn't as likely as me becoming the next Doctor Who.

'You know, some people consider it rude to sleep while the person gracious enough to do the driving sits without conversation for hours on end.'

'Would they also consider it rude if I took out my knife and sliced open their scrotum?'

Kirklander swallowed. 'They, uh, might, yeah.'

I stepped out of the Mini and Kirklander joined me, pointing the way. 'That's it,' he said, indicating a small, stone, humpback bridge arching over a narrow river.

'Right, come on then.' I strode over the road and made my way across the grass and down towards the bridge, Kirklander at my heel, his staff in one hand, resting on his shoulder.

'You know you snore, right?'

'I don't!' I snapped.

'You do. The whole journey you were making the cutest little snorty, snuffling sounds. It was really quite adorable.'

'Shut up.'

'Like a kitten with a cold.'

I stopped and turned on him, fists clenched. 'Do I always snore?'

Kirklander frowned. 'Hard to say. I'm usually asleep by then because of all the very energetic and long-lasting love-making.'

I already said *uuurrrgghhh,* didn't I? I should really have saved it for this point. My fault.

I turned back to the bridge and ran my hands along its large grey stones. Each was worn with age and mottled with moss and other vegetation. It was the kind of bridge that, if this were a fairy tale, you might find a troll living beneath. This wasn't a fairy tale, of course, but trolls did exist. They tended to prefer basement flats to dank bridges, though, and who could blame them?

I stooped low to get under the bridge and waved for Kirklander to follow. A thin, grassy bank on either side of the rushing river allowed us to clamber beneath it without getting our feet wet. Which was just as well, as the last thing we needed was to walk in water. No, we needed to walk *on* it.

'There,' said Kirklander, pointing with his staff, the end of which glowed brightly, cutting through the gloom.

'I see it,' I replied. On the underside of the bridge was a mark: an 'H', carved into the stone. 'This is the spot.'

I turned to the river and took a breath.

To get to the Hidden Forest, you had to go beneath the

bridge and, at the point marked, step into the water. If you did so, and believed in your destination, your foot wouldn't break the water's surface. It would carry your weight. You could then walk forward and, instead of emerging on the other side of the bridge and into the fields beyond, you would find yourself walking into a forest.

'As with orgasms,' said Kirklander, 'ladies first.'

'You must be thinking of some other lady,' I replied as I stepped off the bank and into the river. I was happy to discover that I wasn't engulfed by the water and whisked away by the flow. Instead, I stood impossibly on the river.

'Jesus got nothing on me, boy,' I said.

Kirklander stepped down to join me. 'Shame, I was rather looking forward to getting you wet.'

'Okay, that's the last one, you hear me?'

Kirklander grinned and raised his hands. 'Scout's honour. Now, let's go somewhere creepy.' He shuffled forward, still having to crouch, and I followed.

Within a few steps we straightened up, the bridge gone, the river gone too. Now we were stood among tall grass and ferns in a dark, thickly-wooded area.

The Hidden Forest.

I turned to look in the direction we'd come from. The bridge was still there, the way out. The river was there too, flowing underneath it, but instead of continuing its journey on this side of the bridge, the water just stopped as though it had struck an invisible wall. The water didn't flow into this place, into this secret forest. Here it just cut off, allowing me to step out of the water and directly on to dry ground.

I returned my attention to our new surroundings. Kirklander hadn't been lying, the Hidden Forest was creepy looking as fuck. All around us were giant, twisted, gnarled trees that reached up and up, the canopy so dense that it blotted out the sky.

'Okay, come on.' I said, walking deeper into the forest, fallen twigs cracking beneath my boots like rifle shots.

'Is it just me, or are there... things watching us?' asked Kirklander.

His hand white-knuckled his magic staff. It wasn't just him. My skin was crawling too. I felt eyes on me, but each time I turned to look at what was spying on us, the eyeballs bled into the darkness or darted away.

'This place plays tricks on you, you know that,' I said, and wondered how convincing I'd sounded. I'd not been to the place before, but we'd both heard about how it could affect you.

'Yeah, I know.'

It was true, people had been known to go mad exploring the Hidden Forest. It seeped its way into your mind. It could make you believe dreadful things. It could make you do unforgivable things. And it could make you say all sorts of awful things.

Awful things like: 'I really fancy you.'

'What?' replied Kirklander, genuinely surprised.

'Nothing,' I replied, wondering why I'd just said that. I mean, it was true, I did fancy him, but he was the last person I needed to know that.

'It sounded like you said something.'

'Well, I didn't, and I certainly didn't say that I want you inside me all the time.' I slapped my hand over my mouth, horrified.

'I *definitely* heard that.' He hooted, thoroughly pleased with himself. 'Talking of sex, did you know I actually lost my virginity aged twenty-two and cried so much after that the woman left and never answered her phone again?'

Kirklander's face fell, his eyes so wide I thought his eyeballs might drop out of their sockets. Yeah, I burst out laughing.

'You told me you lost it to your dinner lady when you were still a kid!'

'I did! Didn't! Did! Didn't! What the hell is going on?'

'It's this place,' I said, worried about what might tumble out of my treacherous mouth next. 'You know you really hurt me when you left me behind and let me get arrested.'

Bollocks.

'I hate myself for doing that and I miss you,' replied Kirklander.

Well.... shit.

'Wait, is that true? And is that you saying that, or this place forcing it?'

Kirklander sighed and ran his hands through his thick, dark hair. 'Look, I... shh!'

'What?'

He put a finger to his lips and pointed past me. I turned to see we'd been joined by a huge deer with a very unique-looking set of antlers sprouting from its head. This was the real way to reach Gjindor. He wasn't in the Hidden Forest itself, but the way to reach his realm lived here. A deer with antlers shaped like upside-down crucifixes.

'Your name is Erin Banks,' said the deer in a deep, sonorous voice.

'Talking deer,' said Kirklander. 'Okay.'

'Your name is Elric Cuthbert Kirklander.'

'Cuthbert?' I said with a smirk.

'Shut up.'

'I am the path, the way, the link,' said the deer.

I stepped slowly towards the deer. As I got closer I saw that the antlers were stained a dark red. Blood.

'We seek passage to Gjindor's realm. Will you let us pass?'

The deer's head tilted to one side, its entirely black eyes regarding me quizzically.

'Perhaps. Most who ask do not return to walk through this forest and find the bridge again. Most remain in Gjindor's realm, their bones and flesh and brains crunched between his many teeth before what's left is swallowed.'

'Sounds like a party,' said Kirklander.

The deer's head twitched, turning its attention to my companion. 'You, he would not swallow. Gjindor would chew and chew, enjoying your screams, before spitting your mangled remains into the dirt.'

'I'm starting to like the sound of this demon,' I said.

'I bet I taste great, too,' grumbled Kirklander.

He did, but since I seemed to be in control of my mouth again, there was no way he was going to hear that from me.

The deer regarded us both. 'Best turn around and walk away from this secret place, yes? While you still have legs to walk with.'

'No,' I replied, 'we wish an audience with the demon, Gjindor.'

The deer snorted and fresh blood began to weep from its antlers, dripping down to splash upon its head and face. 'You are quite sure that you will not see sense and run from this forest?'

'Damn skippy.'

The deer shook its head, blood spraying the vegetation around it. This was all a ritual. The steps that needed to be taken that Cupid had laid out to us. Questions that had to be asked, and answers that had to be given to open the door to Gjindor's realm.

'Then once more, you must tell me,' said the deer, 'what is your desire?'

'Grant us entrance, grant us witness,' I replied.

'It is done,' said the deer.

Behind it stood a stone arch with a wooden door that hadn't been there before. It looked as though it had belonged to an old cottage, the rest of which had crumbled, leaving behind a doorway and nothing more.

'Are you ready for this?' I asked Kirklander. 'We're probably going to get our arses handed to us through there.'

'Don't worry about me,' he replied, 'danger is my middle name.'

'I thought it was Cuthbert?'

Kirklander grimaced and walked towards the entrance to the demon's realm.

15

The wind was vicious in Gjindor's realm. It didn't just gently ruffle your hair, it was a whip that bit into your flesh, rasping you raw.

'What a dump,' said Kirklander, twirling his staff in one hand like he was trying out for the Majorettes.

Together, we gazed out across the world we'd stepped into. I can't say I disagreed with him. Gjindor's realm was a harsh, desolate place. The ground was barren, scorched rock without a whisper of green to break up the dull monotony. Dotted here and there like pimples on a backside were the burnt, brittle husks of tree stumps. It was like some giant *Game of Thrones* monster had scorched the place clean. I glanced up at the sky for any sign of a swooping dragon, just in case. I was fairly certain that dragons didn't really exist, but then this realm was a step beyond what I was used to. We were in a different, more dangerous place now than the Uncanny Kingdom.

This wasn't Britain, or Europe, or technically any place on Earth. This was a demon's realm, its personal hidey hole, where it lurked silently, ready to lunge into my world and claim its next victim like a trapdoor spider from Hell.

'How big do you reckon this place is?' asked Kirklander, turning in a circle, 'because it looks pretty samey, and for all we know goes on for miles in every direction. I'll be honest with you, I am not a big fan of hiking.'

'Fuck should I know?' I responded.

He was right, though. The demon's realm could stretch out for hundreds, even thousands, of miles, and the rotten bastard could be lurking anywhere within it. With no clear direction to head in, nothing distinguishing one barren vista from the next, we could easily head off in the wrong direction and not know for days.

Awesome.

A brittle tree trump exploded, scattering splinters like a claymore. Kirklander lowered his staff, the end still glowing with the residue of the magic he'd unleashed.

'What did you do that for, you dick?' I asked, picking bits off wood out of my hair. 'More target practice?'

'Just leaving a marker for the return journey,' he replied. 'So we know where the exit is.'

'Right. And you don't think that big door there, the one standing upright in the middle of nowhere, might also give us a clue?'

'You can never be too sure,' he replied, a little embarrassed. 'I say we go that way.' He pointed his staff in his favoured direction, so I, of course, headed off in the opposite one.

'Hey, wait a sec,' said Kirklander, hustling across the craggy ground to join me.

We'd walked for almost an hour before he said it.

'Should have gone my way.'

'Do you want me to punch you?'

Kirklander considered the question for a few seconds. 'Depends. Sometimes that leads to sex. Will it lead to sex?'

'We're walking across one of the most dangerous places imaginable, a demon's realm, and you're wondering if we're going to bone? We could be picked off at literally any second.'

'So that's a "maybe"?'

'You're an idiot, you know that?'

'You've told me often enough, so I guess there must be some truth in it. Oh... shit.'

'What?'

I followed the direction Kirklander was now pointing his staff. It was the tree stump he'd destroyed. A little way to the left stood the open door, the Hidden Forest beyond it.

'Shit.'

'Is it possible we walked in a big circle?' asked Kirklander.

'No. It knows we're here. It's playing with us.'

'Well, that's not at all worrying. Look how not worried I am, baby.'

I didn't look. 'Come on.'

I stalked off in another direction. It was likely pointless, but I wasn't the type to sit and wait. Staying on the move fooled me into thinking I had some control over the situation and not just waiting for the hammer to fall.

Gjindor knew we were here. I mean, that was no great surprise, most demons could feel the twitch of the web when someone new entered their realm.

So we walked.

Walked for hours and hours, passing the open doorway, the splintered tree stump, over and over. Maybe Gjindor was never going to show up, was just going to let us walk ourselves into exhaustion and pass out. Bit of a bitch move, if you ask me.

'I meant to ask...' said Kirklander.

'No, I'm not going to reach into your pocket and grab myself a treat.' Fallen for that one before.

'No, not that, not this time. I was just going to ask how your mum was doing.'

I stopped in my tracks and turned to face Kirklander, as surprised by him as I'd ever been. 'What did you say?'

'Your mum, she's in hospital, right?'

I actually felt a little light-headed. This line of questioning, where was it coming from?

'Yeah, she's in hospital. How did you know that?'

'Because you're my girl.'

'I'm not, but carry on.'

'I keep an eye on you. On your life. Plus, Lana phoned me.'

'You fucking what?' First of all, the idea that those two had any sort of contact boggled my mind, secondly, how dare she take it upon herself to spread my private business around town?

'She cares about you, that's all.'

'How does she even know you?' I asked.

'Oh, a little while back she turned up at my door. I thought she was the girl I'd ordered, but no. Anyway, she barges her way inside, all red-faced and blonde-haired, and started tearing strips off me. Said you'd told her all about me.'

'I did not!' Unless I was drunk. I say a lot when I'm drunk. Yeah, I definitely did. Bollocks. A sudden, hazy image of me sobbing on Lana's shoulder about how Kirklander had broken my heart swam into view, and I wished very hard for Gjindor to open the rocky earth beneath my feet and swallow me up.

'Anyway, I ended up charming her,' he shrugged, 'it's a curse. We swapped numbers and she calls from time to time. I think it helps her to have someone else to talk to about all the stuff you do. The stuff that scares her.'

Way to make me feel bad, Lana. That woman had been busy. First Parker, now Kirklander in her contact list. Not sure I was entirely happy about that. Actually, I was sure I wasn't.

'She thinks I'm no good for you, by the way. Can you imagine?'

'Yeah, she's a great judge of character.'

Kirklander laughed. 'Smoking hot, too.'

'She's married.'

'And?'

'And I'll cut off your dick and feed it to the gulls.'

'Understood. So, how is she? Your mother?'

I grimaced and started walking again. Was I really going to have this conversation? Here? With *him*?

'She's okay.'

Huh, it looked as though I was.

'That's good.'

'Is it?'

'Yes? Or no. I don't know. You don't talk about your parents much. Or at all, really.'

'Lana is my only family.'

What was this? Kirklander pretending he cared about my emotional wellbeing? That he actually had a heart? I had enough going on without adding that mind fuck to the mix. This was the same man that had run out on me when I wasn't even capable of even standing up, leaving me at the mercy of the police and a three year jail sentence. The same man that had only recently tried to muscle me out of a case I was on, stealing a dagger and getting in between me and an errant soul. The same man that had made me feel on fire, that had made me feel safe and normal when his arm was around me and our naked bodies were one.

'You can talk to me, you know,' said Kirklander. No swagger in his voice, no sarcasm. He sounded, sort of... sincere.

'No. I can't. And I won't.'

I felt his hand touch my arm and I stopped walking, my heart thudding against my chest, the wind of Gjindor's realm doing its best to push me towards him.

'I wouldn't have left you in there. In prison.'

I turned and looked up at him, into those big, green eyes of his. And for perhaps the first time, I think I saw the real Kirklander. The Kirklander who wasn't playing a character. Who was hiding behind the fool. It was a Kirklander I didn't know existed. Or was this just another game? Another con to get me back into his bed?

'Sooner or later, I would've got you out of there, I promise.'

'You promise? That's a laugh.'

My body was at war with itself. Anger trying to stamp out hope, fear in a stand-off with lust. Or maybe it was love.

Shit.

Why was he doing this?

I felt him turn me further towards him. I didn't fight it, didn't pull away.

'I'm not a good person,' he said, 'not even close. But the thing I said to you that night, I meant it.'

'I don't know what you're talking about.'

'I could spend the rest of my life with you.' Yeah, okay stupid memory, I remember what he said, why don't you?

A polite cough killed the moment.

We turned to see a figure perched upon one of the black-ened tree stumps, puffing on a long-stemmed pipe, blowing out a thick cloud of grey smoke.

'You have entered the lair of the Dark One. Prepare to die horribly.'

As I pulled away from Kirklander and our awkward conversation, I'd never been so happy that my life was being threatened.

16

W e spread out, Kirklander heading left, me right, our eyes locked on the figure who remained still and relaxed, the uppermost point of the invisible triangle we'd created.

'Gjindor?' I asked, my tattoos burning bright with power as magic soaked into them, sharpening my senses, filling me with the desire to hurt, to hunt, to kill.

'I know you're only a minor demon,' said Kirklander, the tip of his staff pulsing with a multi-coloured magical flame, 'but I hadn't expected you to be such a short-arse.'

The creature kept puffing on his Gandalf pipe. It was skinny and grey, its skin moist like a snail's. On top of his squat neck sat a large, bulbous head that was home to a mouthful of sharp teeth, the remains of a nose that looked like it had been half-bitten off, and two large, black eyes that bugged from their sockets.

No, this wasn't the demon, this was just one of its helpers. Most demons had worshippers, lackeys, emissaries, even a minor demon like Gjindor. Slithering turds that scampered around the Satan wannabes.

'Okay ugly, where's your master?' I asked, pulling a dagger from my belt. 'I'd like to introduce his guts to my knife, here.'

The creature laughed. Not a mocking or cruel laugh. I'd genuinely tickled the gross little guy.

'Gjindor is the bringer of fear. Gjindor is he who frightens those that cannot be frightened. Gjindor is the one that Mr. Cotton and Mr. Spike have nightmares about.'

'We get it, you little freak,' said Kirklander, 'you're his full-time dick rider. Now where is the prick?'

I didn't see the creature move, but suddenly he was stood before Kirklander. He lashed out, his fist meeting Kirk's stomach and causing him to double over, gasping. Then, in the time it took to blink, he was sat nonchalantly on the stump again, puffing away on his pipe.

'Nippy little bastard,' said Kirklander, his face red, panting for air.

I fixed my eyes on the creature, my hand tight around the handle of my knife, my body full of fury waiting to be unleashed.

'Why don't you try that with me, you ugly little—'

—A punch I didn't see landed me on my arse. The bastard had a mean jab. I got up, the creature still sat upon the stump, relaxed as you like.

'My name is Holland,' said the creature. 'I will take you to Gjindor so that he may pluck your limbs from their sockets and feast upon your screams.'

'Yeah, thanks, appreciate it,' I replied, rubbing my jaw, wondering if the little fucker had fractured it.

Holland hopped from the flaking tree stump and walked away from us.

'I've decided I don't like you, Holland,' said Kirklander, following on.

'I will like it when you are naked and broken and covered in your own piss and sick and shit, quivering before the exquisite darkness of my master,' replied Holland. 'You will cry and crawl and the evil one will tear your penis from betwixt your legs and feed it to you. A small meal.'

'Jesus. Bit strong,' said Kirklander, tossing a look my way.

'I'm starting to like him,' I replied, striding at Kirklander's side.

We followed behind Holland and his ever-present cloud of smoke. As we walked, something strange started to happen. Instead of walking through an endless rocky, scorched expanse as before, the world around us seemed to shift and warp every few steps. Sometimes, I'd look around and realise we were actually underground, squeezing our way through narrow, damp tunnels that opened up into vast, cathedral-like caves full of enormous, crystal stalactites that reached down from a ceiling too high to see.

A few more steps and the view would peel like an orange, and now we'd be making our way through what looked like a long-abandoned medieval town, home only to rats the size of large dogs. Rats that huddled in the empty stone buildings, their yellow teeth chattering, shining eyes watching our progress.

'I feel sick,' said Kirklander as the rat town spun away and we stepped into a long-abandoned fairground, the rides and stalls degraded, rusted, claimed by hungry vegetation. It was a disorientating process, the journey the little grey bastard was taking us on, and I could feel my stomach churning, travel sick.

Holland stopped and pointed into the distance with the mouthpiece of his pipe. 'Over there.'

'Where?' I replied, squinting but not seeing any sign of a person, let alone a demon.

'He's gone. Rude little git,' said Kirklander.

I turned in a quick circle. He was right, the lackey had melted away.

'Get ready,' I said, 'if I know demons, things are about to go downhill fast.'

Kirklander grinned and spun his staff from one hand to the other. 'Time to make bank, baby.'

We walked forward. My fists and teeth were clenched, my tattoos glowing, buzzing with Uncanny power. Each footstep caused a mini-tsunami of dust to erupt from the parched ground as we made our way past the skeletal remains of big wheels and waltzers.

'Heads up,' said Kirklander, nodding towards a stone bench, upon which sat a lone figure.

'I found this place in the memory of a woman called Jane,' said the man in the shabby, dusty suit. 'She was very old when I met her. At least, very old for a human. Her skin was like damp wallpaper, so easy to tear.'

Demons come in all sorts of strange forms. There are giants like the Long Man, that look like something from a monster movie. Then there are others that could almost pass for human.

'As I stripped away her skin, her meat, her veins, and arranged them in a neat pile in the dirt, I took a wander through her memories. That's where I found the fairground. A deceased place that would once have echoed with noise and laughter and pop-pop-popcorn.'

Gjindor looked like someone you might find huddled, hollow-eyed, in a back alley doorway. Malnourished, dressed in a suit he'd worn every day for years, his hair greasy, straggly, and sparse. Sores were scattered across his face like the tree stumps across this barren realm.

'When Jane found the fairground, during a road trip across America when she was barely thirty years old, it was already long silent. She walked through the place and found herself crying without really knowing why. I liked that memory. So I kept it for myself.'

Gjindor grinned, exposing blackened gums that held a riot of dagger-like, yellow teeth.

A woman with hay coloured hair walked into view, hands clenched to her chest, tears damp on her rosy cheeks. Jane. We watched in silence as she walked past us all, unaware of anything but the dead rides around her, before turning out of view.

'Jesus, that's creepy,' said Kirklander.

'Pussy,' I replied, pretending the hairs on the back of my arms weren't standing on end.

I flinched back as Gjindor stood and turned to face us, his eyes yellow and dried-out, the colour of a tobacco stain on the ceiling above a smoker's favourite chair. I fondled the leather pouch in my pocket. One of those eyes was heading back to Brighton with me.

'So brave to come here,' said the demon. 'I did not think anyone they hired would be so foolish. So stupid.'

'Never underestimate our idiocy,' replied Kirklander, stepping forward, staff pointed at the beast. 'Eat this!' A crackling ball of magic burst from the staff, surging towards the demon.

It did nothing.

Gjindor raised a hand and caught the magic in his fist. He turned it over in the palm of his grubby hand and studied it like it was a bit of fluff he'd plucked from his navel.

'Okay, not the ideal outcome,' said Kirklander, lowering his staff.

'Would you like it back?' asked Gjindor.

'No, that's fine,' replied Kirklander, 'you keep it.'

With a grimace, Gjindor threw the ball of strobing magic back towards him at such a speed it was impossible to get out of the way. It struck Kirklander full-force in the chest, lifted him off his feet, and tossed him over the wrought iron fence of the collapsing fair, and out of sight.

'Kirklander!' I yelled, but he didn't reply.

'Memories,' said Gjindor, 'my sister and I do enjoy the forgotten days of others. Enjoy reaching into the pictures of times gone by.'

'Not really here for your family history, fuck face.' Tattoos burning, muscles begging to be put to use, I charged forward, knife in hand. The magic coursing through my body made me fast, made me brave, made me ignore the lunacy of charging head-first at a demon.

The old fair twisted, the world turned, and I fell to the dusty dirt.

Wait, no, it wasn't dusty, my hands and knees were pressed against a carpeted floor. I knew that floor. Which was daft, how could I know a place just from the close-up of a floor I hadn't seen since I was a child? Since before all the bad stuff. But I did, the recollection was instant.

I was in a caravan. The door was open to the green field outside, and I could smell bacon, could hear it crackling in a pan. My dad was cooking breakfast on the camping stove outside and whistling an old Kinks song. *Waterloo Sunset*.

I stood as my mum stepped in from the field, the caravan rocking slightly as she climbed inside.

'Hey doodle-bug,' she said. Said to *me*. 'Up at last? Breakfast is nearly done.' She was smiling at me. Is that what she looked like when she was happy? When she didn't have that loss crushing her? When her eyes weren't full of silent accusations?

She looked young.

Alive.

Full of colour.

I thought about the last time I'd seen her, laid up in a hospital bed. A husk. Muted. Someone who'd been going through the motions for decades but whose spark had long ago been snuffed out.

'Mum?' I wanted to step forward, to hug her, to turn her shoulder damp with my tears. That look in her eyes wasn't accusing, wasn't empty, it was loving. She adored me, her eyes practically screamed it, and it overwhelmed me. I staggered back, the seating behind me striking my calves, causing me to drop down and sit, heart hammering.

'So vivid, this memory,' said Gjindor, who was now sat next to me. 'This is your perfect moment. The place you've been wanting to go back to your whole life.'

'Get out of my head,' I said, trembling.

'I could let you live here forever. Or what'll be left of you. The *idea* of you. The last gasp of your soul. Forever here, like Jane, wandering through her abandoned fairground. Would that be kind? Would that be good?'

'Why are you doing this?'

'Because it is my nature. Because I can. Because my family is one with the memories of others. Because you walked into my realm with murder in mind.'

My dagger was still gripped in my hand.

My dad stepped into the caravan holding a plate piled high with sandwiches made of thick-cut white bread, crisp bacon, and brown sauce.

I twisted and thrust the knife into Gjindor's heart.

Only it didn't find its target, instead it juddered to a stop as it found the leg of the table I was now sat underneath.

'I believe you,' said Lana, hugging her knees, eleven years old, eyes wide and wanting nothing more but to comfort me, help me, make me know I wasn't alone.

I saw Gjindor's battered shoes, one sole hanging off, step into view beyond the tablecloth that hung low, hiding Lana and me from our parents.

'Why are you standing as a witness?' I asked him.

'Should the guilty not be punished?' he replied.

'I believe in monsters, too,' said Lana, as I yanked my knife from the table leg and crawled out from under the table, pushing the cloth aside.

'Demons tend not to follow the due course of the law, in my experience,' I told Gjindor.

The room around me was faded, half-formed, some of the details hazy and unfinished. It seemed my mind hadn't retained the minutiae of the kitchen as clearly as they had the holiday caravan.

'When found guilty of her dreadful crimes, the punishment for Liyta will be death,' said Gjindor. 'A dark wizard will reach into her chest and crush her heart. As her soul looks down upon her lifeless body, the wizard will claim it, shred it, make her less than nothing.'

'Yeah, but usually your type like to do that themselves, not sit around and give evidence.'

Gjindor smiled, a split tongue teasing out from between his crooked jumble of teeth.

'What are you hiding?'

The tablecloth lifted and Lana poked her head out. 'Quick, under here before anyone sees you!'

I thrust my knife forward, hoping to sink it into Gjindor's stomach, but instead found empty air. I fell to my knees, collapsing not on the tiles of the kitchen floor, but on thick, warm carpet. It was a dark brown carpet with swirls of lighter brown woven through it.

It was the carpet of the home I grew up in. I looked up to see I was in the hallway. Outside the doors to the bedrooms. My parents. Mine. My brother's.

'Is he in there, or has he already been taken?' asked Gjindor.

I felt like I was going to be sick. 'I'm going to kill you,' I said.

Gjindor laughed and clapped his hands together. 'I believe I shall play with you for a very long time.'

I wanted to open the door to James' room. To step in and see him. Was it already too late to save him? To protect him from the Red-Eyed Man?

'Are you too scared to tell me why you're doing it then? Why you're so eager for Liyta to face the Uncanny Court? Don't get me wrong, the bitch deserves it, but your part in this makes no sense. Sorta beneath something like you, I'd say.'

Gjindor grimaced. That had got to him. My blade had yet to reach its target, but those words had hit home all right.

'She is an abomination.'

'Agreed,' I replied, 'but that's a bit rich, coming from a bloke with your dentistry.'

Gjindor's head tilted as he regarded me. A slight nod before he went on. 'A high demon and a wretched, mortal woman fell in love. The woman bore a child. That child was Liyta. A half-breed.'

'So why not kill the bitch yourself?'

'A demon cannot raise a hand against their own family, nor order their murder.'

'Did you just say "family"?' And that's when things slotted into place. 'Liyta is your half-sister. Holy shit.'

Gjindor snarled, anger showing on his face for the first time. 'No half-breed abomination is my family. She is a stain on our house and I will not stand for it. I will testify, she will face the justice of the dark wizard, and the bad taste shall be washed from my mouth.'

Jesus. Family issues ran deep in all of us, it seemed. Even demons.

I couldn't say the two looked similar, but one thing connected them. Memory. I remembered how Liyta was able to tease out bits of my past as she looked at me. Her power clearly wasn't on the same level as her brother's— probably weakened by only being half-demon—but they clearly shared a family gift.

'So you're going to lower yourself to a day in court because the idea of having a half-human sister makes you feel a bit icky?'

'She is wrong. She is a disgrace. The bastard child must be stamped out.'

Now? Now. He was distracted, his emotions boiling over. Time for attempt three. I lunged forward but the corridor spiralled away from me again. I found myself in Other London once more. Not the Other London I'd visited recently, where I'd spoken with Carlisle and almost died. No, this was the Other London I'd found myself in as a child, running after the things that took my brother. It looked much larger now, the buildings looming higher than they had on my last visit; a child's view of the world.

'This is where they took him,' said Gjindor. 'The fallen place. Your memories are interesting to me. Someone has tried to hide things from you.'

The magic Carlisle mentioned had been used to scramble events. To hide that night from us.

'Can you see?' I asked, stepping towards the demon, this time my thoughts not turning to stabbing him. 'Can you walk me through the things that were hidden?'

'A child. A talking pig. A creature with red eyes. Little James, taken away into the night to a secret place where magic paved the very streets, but for what purpose?'

'Tell me. Tell me and I'll leave your realm. I'll stop anyone else from even attempting to come here to kill you. I promise.'

'The promise of an assassin? I think not.'

He was here. Somewhere in this memory, James was hiding. If the demon wouldn't show me, I'd look myself. Find where he went, find what happened. I turned my back on Gjindor and ran, yelling my brother's name. I raced along street after street, looking for the pig, looking for the dark figure with burning red eyes, looking for my baby brother, held aloft in a ball of magic.

'And just what do we have here, wandering these hidden streets?'

I turned to see Carlisle stepping out of the shadows.

'Help me! Help me find him!' I cried, grabbing Carlisle by his coat, only for him to turn to smoke and drift apart, revealing Gjindor stood in his place.

'I see it all,' he said, a smile stretching wider and wider across his face, his sores cracking and weeping. 'I see the whole story and the truth behind it. How delicious.'

'Please. I have to know. Please, tell me.'

'Kneel. Kneel and beg me, and I shall tell you.'

I don't kneel. Not for anyone. Not ever.

'Kneel and beg me, child.'

I felt astonishment and betrayal wash over me as I

realised my body was doing just as the demon asked. I slowly dropped to my knees, my hair hanging down to cover my face. The words slipped from my mouth, stinging my lips. 'Please. I beg you.'

Gjindor laughed and I felt myself sag, my hands meeting the floor to hold me up, to stop me from curling up in a ball.

'I will not, worm,' replied Gjindor with a smirk.

I was going to kill him. Not for the money, not because it was my job, not because he was a demon. I was going to kill him because it would make me feel good.

Shame gone, weakness banished, I leapt to my feet, tattoos blazing, knife gripped in hand, ready to die if that's what it took to end the smirking fucker.

And then a hand reached out of nowhere and pressed a magical charm to Gjindor's forehead. It met the demon's flesh with a sharp sizzle, and the demon recoiled, screaming, as the world around us melted away.

'Yeah, that's what you get for fucking me up with my own fuck-you-up magic!' cried Kirklander, his clothes torn, face bloodied.

My memory fell apart immediately, replaced with the reality of the demon's realm, the endless expanse of scorched, barren rock and blackened tree stumps.

'What was that?'

Kirklander opened his coat to reveal all sort of charms fixed to the inside. 'I'm a professional, babe. Think I go walking into a demon's realm without a shit-tonne of protection?'

Gjindor screamed as he tore the charm from his forehead, the charm ripping a hunk of cooked flesh away with it.

'You will—' his yellow, sickly eyes widened with surprise as my blade punctured his side.

'How'd you like that, fuck-face?' I whispered in his ear.

With a cry, Gjindor swung out with the back of one hand, my jaw breaking as he hit home, sending me spinning away through the air. I landed with a painful crash, my body demolishing a whole row of tree stumps as I ploughed a long line through the ashy ground. And this was only a minor demon.

'You think a knife can stop me?' Gjindor roared. 'I am the bringer of darkness!' He pulled the blade from his side and it crumbled to dust in his hand. He stomped towards me and reached out a hand, ready to take my skull in his grimy grip and crush it to pieces. Fortunately for me, a wall of magic burst from Kirklander's staff and knocked Gjindor off his feet.

'How about that, eh, chuckles?' he said, and I'd never wanted him more.

By way of a response, Gjindor tore a tree stump from the ground and launched it in Kirklander's direction. Kirk spun on the spot, staff pointing to the ground, trying to form a quick circle of protection. He almost completed the ward, but not quite. A shard of wood penetrated the bubble and opened a gash in his side. With an agonised scream, he fell to the ground.

'Kirk!'

'You are a halfling abomination, too,' said Gjindor, whirling about to me. 'A mortal grafting magic onto her unclean flesh.'

As my tattoos fixed my broken jaw, I grabbed a splintered chunk of the stump I'd destroyed and lunged for Gjindor, desperate to feel it sink into his flesh. He swatted the shard aside and gripped me by the throat, lifting me from the ground as I struggled, kicked out, yelled in fury.

'Another bitch hybrid for the slaughter,' said Gjindor, his serpent's tongue snaking out from between his blistered lips to trace a sticky passage across my cheek.

I spat in his face and found myself landing in a heap several metres away, the wind knocked from my lungs.

It was stupid of me to think I could walk into a demon's realm, even a minor demon like Gjindor, and finish on top. Finish with me plucking an eyeball from his corpse. Because he was right, I was just a mortal who wore magic like a kid wears a transfer tattoo. I was strong, quick, vicious, but that wasn't enough.

'Oh, shit,' said Kirklander, staggering over to me, leaning on his staff for support.

'Yeah, we're going to die. Sucks, right?'

'No, no, not that... that!'

I turned to where Kirklander was pointing. It was the door. The exit that would led us to the Hidden Forest and away from this place.

But it wasn't the door itself he was pointing at, it was what was coming through it.

A shadow with nothing to cast it crept along the rocky surface of Gjindor's realm. And then a second, a third, a fourth. The prosecution's attack dogs. The shades. They'd caught up, followed our scent, and crept through the door we'd left open. They'd followed us cross-country, never tiring, relentless, starving, and at last they had caught up.

Well, shit.

The shades gathered around Gjindor.

'You shall not touch them,' he told them. 'I am Gjindor. This realm is mine, and so are their deaths, their memories, their pain.'

The shades bristled around him, writhed over each other, desperate to attack as they had been ordered. To latch on to us and tear our bodies to pieces. They wouldn't be denied the taste of death, especially when they were so close to it. One shade darted forward and Gjindor snarled, causing the shadow to halt, to retreat, to thrash with fury.

'Erin,' said Kirklander.

'Yes?'

'I think I've got an idea.'

'If you make some sort of sex joke at this point I'm going to beat you to death with your own shoe.'

'Not a sex joke. A plan.'

'Is it make a run for the door?'

'It has run in it, but not that. How fast do you think you can go?'

'Fast enough.'

'You'll need to be faster than that.'

'Why?'

'Piggyback time.'

Ah.

Now, most of you would stop to question this instruction, but this wasn't mine and Kirklander's first time at the races. I knew exactly what he meant.

And so I slowed my breathing. I needed to be the best I could be. Needed to be better than that. Straining, I reached out. Called out. My tattoos ached as I demanded more and more. Demanded they drench me in the magic around us. And this wasn't your ordinary Uncanny magic. This was the background magic of a demon's realm. This was heavy, old, powerful magic. The kind of magic that could addle your brain if you weren't careful. The kind of magic that could push you further, push you faster, than you thought possible.

The potential.

It overtook me. It owned me.

It was like the rest of the world slowed down. Like I'd stepped into a realm of my own. A new reality. This magic, this demon magic, was making demands I wasn't sure my fragile, human body could handle. But I answered those demands anyway.

Kirklander leapt on my back and I ran.

It was as though he weighed no more than a bag of sugar as my legs carried us forward, carried us towards the demon and the shadows that surrounded him. The world was a juddering blur, a slow motion video cassette that had degraded after too many viewings.

The tip of Kirklander's staff met the rock beneath our feet and magic pulsed down it, impregnating the earth as we circled the demon. Gjindor realised what we were doing, but it was too late, I was too fast. His hand reached for me, but I was already gone. It was all over in seconds. The circle complete. A circle of protection that trapped the demon and the shadows, too.

I collapsed to the ground, shaking, Kirklander falling away from me. I couldn't breathe. My body screamed and shook with pain. I'd asked too much of it, let the magic of this place push me too far. Maybe it would kill me.

I felt a hand around my shoulders, levering me into a sitting position. Kirklander was talking to me, I could see his lips moving, but I couldn't hear him. All I heard was a roar in my ears. It wasn't the roar of this realm's raging winds though. It was the sound of my soul screaming.

'...okay? Hey, can... hear...? Erin? Are... okay?'

The wind died and my lungs began to work again. I gulped down great lungfuls of air.

'Shit... shit plan...' I managed to say, as my all-over tremble started coming under control. I grabbed Kirklander's arm and let him help me back to my feet, my teeth clenching as my clothes rubbed painfully against my skin. It felt as though I had the worst sunburn imaginable.

But I was alive.

Just about.

It looked as though I'd pushed things as far as I possibly could. Any more and I'd have shut down completely. Talk about living on the edge.

'This ward will not last,' said Gjindor, the palms of his hands pressed against the invisible barrier Kirklander had created. 'You are a low wizard and your magic is weak. This circle will crumble within minutes, and when it does I will find you. Wherever you run, wherever you hide, I will visit you and deliver pain the likes of which you cannot imagine.'

'More painful than listening to you go on and on?' I asked. I would have smiled as Gjindor snarled and bashed his hands against the barrier, only using the muscles in my face that much would have made me scream.

'We should get out of here,' said Kirklander, not without reason.

'What about his eye? The bounty?'

'I think the ship has sailed on that, don't you?'

'...Find you. Make you scream for all eternity. Will not let you die. Not ever. Pain until the Universe fades to naught.'

'Wait...' I said.

'I still prefer "run away",' replied Kirklander.

'Look. Look at the shadows.'

Rabid dogs. That's what Parker had called them. Dangerous, unpredictable, hungry. They'd been given a job and now, so close, they were trapped. Prevented from tearing us apart. Mere moments from tasting death, and they'd been stopped. They could see us but couldn't do a thing about it.

'Oh,' replied Kirklander, catching on. 'You don't think they're gonna...?'

'Yeah, I really do.'

Gjindor backed away as the shadows writhed and thrashed, but he had nowhere to go.

'Do not dare. I am Gjindor. Stay back!'

Was that fear? I'd never seen a frightened demon before. First time for everything.

'Sorry, ugly, looks like you've been locked in a kennel with a pack of hungry dogs, and these dogs are *hungry*.'

The shades had been denied supper for a week, and Gjindor's flesh would taste as good as anyone's. I thought back to the man I'd bumped into outside of Parker's. How the shades hadn't just passed over him, ignored him, they'd been distracted, their lust for death high, and had started attacking him. Well, now here they were, so close to their two targets, now trapped with someone else. They needed to take their hunger, their lust, their fury out on someone. The demon would have to do for now.

'Break the circle!' he begged. 'Break it!'

'Don't think so, bud,' Kirklander replied.

The demon turned to me, his yellow eyes lit with raw panic. 'Let me out and I'll tell you everything! I'll tell you why your brother was taken!' Gjindor's back was pressed against the invisible barrier as the shadows edged ever closer. 'I know why, I saw it all! I can help you, I promise!'

'The promise of a demon?' I said. I can't say I didn't feel tempted, though. Because I believed him. Just like the Long Man, he'd seen inside my hidden past and he knew something. Maybe knew all of it.

If I helped him, perhaps I'd finally know the truth.

Or perhaps he'd just tear my head off.

Kirklander's hand took mine gently. 'Erin...'

'I will tell you,' said Gjindor. 'I will tell you everything if you release me now.'

I stepped towards the demon, a snarl spread across my face. 'Get on your knees and beg me.'

Gjindor's eyes grew wide.

'Kneel. And beg me.'

The shadows moved as one, latching on to Gjindor. He shook and screamed and raged, but he did not have the power to keep them at bay. They lunged again and again, taking him apart piece by piece, overwhelmed by death-lust.

Kirklander pulled me away and we ran for the exit, passing through into the Hidden Forest and slamming the door shut behind us, cutting off the sound of Gjindor's agony. Kirklander aimed his staff at the ground and formed a new circle around the door.

'Buy us a little extra time after that circle in there gives out,' he said.

'I don't think I can make it all the way to the car,' I said, my body still racked with pain, my tattoos all burned out, my mind begging for sleep.

'You won't leave me, will you?' I asked, the words falling from my mouth slurred and furry.

I stumbled, landing hard on the forest floor, my surroundings smeared with Vaseline. I laid there, limp and helpless, my limbs no longer taking orders. The world was a blur now. I heard a murmur of rustling leaves. Kirklander running away? Taking off again, saving his own hide, leaving me to my fate? How could I have let this happen? Kirklander was never going to change. I'd been a fool to give him even an ounce of trust. The man was a snake, a coward, a rotten bastard who only looked out for number one.

So whose arms were those scooping me into the air as the black rose to greet me?

17

For once, Kirklander hadn't betrayed me.

To be honest, I didn't know whether to be surprised or happy about that. To be even more honest, the fact that I felt anything about it at all pissed me off. I couldn't afford to have feelings for that man. For *any* man, but *especially* that one. I refused to allow them to take root. Affection, compassion, love; those were things to be stamped into the dirt. Just because Kirklander had carried me from the Hidden Forest, didn't mean I owed him. He'd lost any claim to me when he left me for dead the first time. I didn't trust him. I never would again. But the fact that we'd pulled this off, and pulled it off as a team... well, I can't deny it made me smile.

Just a little bit.

Shut up. I know, all right? I just said I didn't trust him still, cut me some slack.

A day later, fully recovered after another stint in Parker's torture chair, Kirklander and I strolled into the reception of Jenkins & Jenkins.

Olivia sat sourly behind the desk to greet us, her eyes practically drawing blood. 'Not dead, then?'

'Not this time,' I replied, 'but you never know, one of these days you might get lucky.'

Olivia grimaced and turned to Kirklander. 'Did you lose my number?' she asked.

'I have no idea what this mad woman is on about,' said Kirklander, trying to look innocent.

'They in?' I said, ignoring Kirk and walking towards the closed office door.

'You're supposed to call ahead!' said Olivia.

I shoved open the door and strode in, Kirklander at my heel. Alive Jenkins was tucking into a large bowl of vanilla ice cream at his desk, while Dead Jenkins was trying to ignore him by looking out of the window and brooding.

'Delicious!' said Alive Jenkins, tucking into his bowl. 'I'm celebrating, in case you were wondering. Thanks to you, the case got thrown out due to the prosecution's lack of witnesses.'

'You must be very happy,' I replied.

'Happy? This is my third bowl! Lovely, tasty ice cream. Yummy, yummy, yummy. Do you know, I can't think of anything worse than not being able to enjoy such a delectable treat.'

Dead Jenkins turned from the window. I think he might have been drooling a little. Can ghosts drool?

'Liyta was very pleased,' said Dead Jenkins, doing his best to ignore his brother.

'Hey, I'm famous for my ability to please the ladies,' said Kirklander. Of course he did.

The case against the defence had fallen apart completely. With no witnesses to call upon, Liyta had been released from the Upside-Down Tower and set loose on the streets.

How did I feel about that?

I'd like to say it didn't bother me. I'd done my job, I didn't discriminate against who I helped, good or bad. If the money was there then so was I. But still, this one felt different. A half-demon was back in the world because of me. I wondered how many might die because of my payday. Because I'd taken the job as a bit of distraction from my messed up life. From my broken family.

I took out the leather pouch containing the eye of Jarvis Fuller, the dead magician. I plucked the jellied orb from inside and tossed it into Alive Jenkins' bowl of ice cream like a gruesome cherry.

He frowned and pushed the bowl away. 'Perhaps two bowls is enough. No need to be greedy.'

'We want all the bounty,' I said.

'All?' said Dead Jenkins.

'Did she say *all*?' asked Alive Jenkins.

'All three witnesses were dealt with, and we're the only two you hired left,' said Kirklander. 'The job was done, now play fair and cough up.'

'Play fair?' replied Dead Jenkins. 'The terms of the contract were very clear. Each eyeball retrieved earned whoever delivered it one third of the bounty.'

'All dead or not,' continued Alive Jenkins, 'one eye gets you one third of the pot.'

'We went up against a demon for this job,' I said, pressing my knuckles into his desk.

'A *minor* demon,' replied Dead Jenkins with a sniff.

'How about I get one of my pals to set a minor demon on you, ghosty?' asked Kirklander. 'See how you like it?'

'You're giving us all of the bounty,' I reiterated. 'Every bit of it. Right now.'

Alive Jenkins stood and rounded his desk, hands up, appeasing. 'Please, please, this is undignified. This is not how professionals work.'

'Do you know the odds of us, of anyone, walking out of a demon's realm alive?'

'I'm not a statistician,' said Kirklander, 'but I'd say those odds were long. Even longer than my—'

My elbow met Kirklander's ribs.

'A deal is a deal,' said Alive Jenkins.

'You sure I can't change your mind?' I asked.

'I'm very sure.'

'Okay. Fair enough,' I replied, then stepped forward and jabbed a finger at Alive Jenkins' windpipe. His eyes bulged and his face turned beetroot red as he clutched his neck and fell against his desk, gasping for air.

'Thing is, I'm Erin fucking Banks. If you think you can stop me getting what's mine, then you've got a world of hurt coming your way.'

'How dare you?' roared Dead Jenkins.

'The full amount, or I keep going,' I said, swiping Alive Jenkins across the face with the back of my hand, busting his nose.

'You'll never work for this firm again!' raged the ghost.

'I can live with that. But I can't live with being played for a sucker.'

I grabbed one of Alive Jenkins' fingers.

'No,' he gasped, 'be reasonable.'

'All of the money. Now.'

Dead Jenkins shook his head, so I snapped his brother's finger. The noise he made was like a cat mewling in slow motion.

'She's crazy, dead guy, I'd do as she asks,' said Kirklander.

'Okay, okay, give them the full bounty. Give it to them!' screamed Alive Jenkins.

'Now let's not be too rash,' replied his brother.

'What?'

'It'll look bad if we crumble too quickly. Think of our reputation.'

Dead Jenkins had clearly decided to take advantage of a bad situation.

'Open the safe. Open it you stupid, dead arsehole!'

'Are you in a lot of pain?' Dead Jenkins asked his brother, who just glared at him. He turned to me. 'I think he can take a little more.'

'You dead basta—' the end of the word transformed into an animal howl as I snapped a second finger.

Dead Jenkins smiled and made his way to a large, iron safe. Making his hand solid, he twisted the dial until the door opened. He pulled out a large, fat envelope and tossed it across the room. Kirklander caught it and ripped the thing open before peering inside.

'We good?' I asked, a third finger in hand, ready for the snapping.

A smile spread across Kirklander's face. It was larger than the first time he'd seen me naked. 'Oh, we're very, very good.'

I released Alive Jenkins' hand and patted him on the head. 'Pleasure doing business with you.'

Alive Jenkins slumped to the carpet, cradling his mangled hand.

'You didn't have to let her snap two!' he bawled at his brother.

'Yes, and you didn't have to eat two giant bowls of ice cream in front of me.'

'Keep us in mind for any future jobs,' said Kirklander as we made our way for the door, the sound of Alive Jenkins' very sweary reply following us all the way to the lift.

I pulled my beanie hat low as I lurked in the car park, off to one side of the hospital entrance. Another day had passed since we'd left Gjindor to the mercy of the rabid shades. Liyta had played on my mind a lot since then. I wondered where she was, what she was up to. I wondered what the family of the people whose deaths she'd been responsible for thought about her going free. How they were coping.

I wondered how I was going to spend my cut of the fat bounty I'd earned for helping her.

'Hey,' said Lana, joining me.

'So I hear you and Kirklander are best buddies these days?'

'Oh. Shit. Right. Are you pissed off?'

'Most of the time,' I replied.

'I can kind of see your problem, though. He is really, really, stupidly hot.'

I laughed and nudged her in the ribs with my elbow.

'You know, your mum said the weirdest thing the other day,' she said.

'Really.'

'She told me she had this dream that you came to see her. Only it didn't feel like a dream, according to her.'

'The old cow's obviously losing her marbles,' I replied.

Lana tried to catch my eyes with hers, but I didn't take the bait. 'Okay. That must be it.'

I shuffled back into the shadows as the hospital doors swished open and Mum was wheeled out, my dad steering the chair.

'You could come and say hello,' said Lana. 'Tell her you're glad she's okay.'

I thought about the caravan. The mum I'd seen in my memory. I wondered if that person was still inside her somewhere. If she even remembered being that alive and unburdened with loss. I wondered if she ever thought of me as anyone besides the person who robbed her of a child.

'Rather stick my hand into a bucket full of broken glass, thanks,' I replied.

Lana sighed. 'Are you okay?'

'Amazing.'

'I'd better get over there,' she said, gesturing to my parents who were waiting by Lana's car. She went to leave before pausing and turning back. 'One day they're going to be gone. Don't wait too long for another visit.' She turned and walked away.

***

I sat slouched at the bar of Baker's Pub, four drinks deep and feeling like reheated shit.

'Hey, get you another one?'

I turned to see a face I recognised. I couldn't place it for a moment, and then it hit me. 'Toilet sex guy.'

His eyes widened as he realised who it was he was hitting on. 'Shit, it's you.' He backed away, looking around for any sign of the giant of a man who'd thrown him across a bathroom the last time we met.

'Calm down, it's just me tonight.'

'Right. Okay.'

He paused, unsure of what to do.

'So are you going to hit on me properly or what?' I asked.

'Yeah. No. Do you want me to?'

I sighed, downed my drink, and grabbed his hand, leading him toward the toilets.

'So are we...?'

'Yeah.'

'Right. Good. Thanks.'

Back to where I'd started. Anonymous, bad, alcohol-fuelled sex to distract me for just a little while.

My life is just one unbroken boulevard of green lights, isn't it?

'So what's your name?' he asked.

'Shut up and unbutton.'

And you best believe he did.

LEAVE A REVIEW

Reviews are gold to indie authors, so if you've enjoyed this book, please consider visiting the site you purchased it from and leaving a quick review.

BECOME AN INSIDER

Sign up and receive **FREE UNCANNY KINGDOM BOOKS**. Also, be the **FIRST** to hear about **NEW RELEASES** and **SPECIAL OFFERS** in the **UNCANNY KINGDOM** universe. Just visit:

WWW.UNCANNYKINGDOM.COM

MORE STORIES SET IN THE UNCANNY KINGDOM

The Uncanny Ink Series
Bad Soul
Bad Blood
Bad Justice
Bad Intention
Bad Thoughts
Bad Memories

The Hexed Detective Series
Hexed Detective
Fatal Moon
Night Terrors

The Branded Series
Sanctified
Turned
Bloodline

The London Coven Series
Familiar Magic
Nightmare Realm
Deadly Portent

The Spectral Detective Series
Spectral Detective
Corpse Reviver
Twice Damned

The Dark Lakes Series
Magic Eater
Blood Stones
Past Sins

Strange Stories
Apocalypse Hill

15268781R00099

Printed in Great Britain
by Amazon